Willowdale Road

To Jules, Mandy, and Panch

Families are like branches on a tree.
We grow in different directions, yet our roots remain as one.

- *anonymous*

Willowdale Road

In my eyes, she could do no wrong. She was perfect.   - Eloy

Clara Bella Rose

Part One

Youngster

HOME

*D*ear God, make him stop. I wish he were dead.

I couldn't tell you how many times I had said those words. For years, I repeated them like a chant. That was the only thing that came to mind while I lay there, waiting for him to finish. It became routine, a couple of days each week before school.

In the mornings, I hated being at home alone with him. When he transformed into Rodas, I no longer saw him as my father. He looked different in the mornings. His eyes were darker than usual, his face was sweaty and pale, and his voice was soft.

He lowered his head. With his breath in my ear, and one hand pressed tight over my mouth, he whispered, "Shh, be quiet. You tell no one."

Sometimes, I thought of telling my secret about Rodas, but I couldn't. Not that I was afraid to tell anyone. I wanted to run and tell Mama and Liv. But I feared his threats. He threatened me with never being able to go to Shannon's house again, of hurting someone else instead.

Have you ever prayed for something specific? *Dear God, take Rodas.*

Did you make a wish on a falling star? *I wish he were dead.*

Have you asked God to show you a sign? *Get me out of here.*

His control over me had power and only his death would release me.

Dear God, make him stop. I wish he were dead.

A Safe Place

We stood and filled the aisle, holding our balance as the school bus screeched to a stop.

"These brakes need fixing," Ms. Sue said, as she leaned forward, grasped the handle, and pulled. The doors opened, and we took the last steps toward summer.

"Have a great summer break." Her words came as a wish, and the summer heat walked us home. We were the last stop on the route. While the bus ride was long, the walk home seemed longer.

Of course, Shannon's mom would be there waiting to pick her up. "Sorry, girls, we're heading towards town, or I'd give you a ride," Wanda said.

"That's okay, we like the walk," I lied.

The walk would have been nice any day except today, which was exceptionally hot. Carmen and I kept pace, chatting about the summer and our daily plans. The older kids walked ahead while kicking a dead snake from the street to the grass.

Carroll Pines was a small town north of Tampa, hidden among the orange groves and cow pastures that lined the streets. The bus stop began our one mile walk from the intersection of Citrus Grove and Willowdale Roads. We followed the electric lines and streetlights as they guided us along the dirt road mixed with gravel and broken-down seashells. Tall pine trees and Spanish moss hung as a canopy that provided some shade. Willowdale Road ended where the bend in the half-moon began. Half Moon Lake was what you'd expect, an odd shape of a crescent moon.

"Good afternoon, Vivi. Are you stopping by for a cold one?" Mr.

Powell asked. His Royal Crown Cola machine always had a variety of sodas. The handwritten sign on the machine read: Nickels only. A string tied through a nickel hung out of the slot. I dropped the coin in the slot, opened the glass door, and pulled the lever for the soda I wanted.

"Don't forget to take the nickel out," Mr. Powell reminded me. I enjoyed the sound of the metal cap releasing from the glass bottle: *pop* and *clink* as it fell deep inside the machine. After my long walk, nothing was more satisfying than the cold, sweet drink of an RC quenching my thirst.

"Thanks again, see you tomorrow," I said as I crossed the street towards home.

Daddy removed the iron welding rods from his truck. "Consider yourself lucky that he doesn't make you pay for those sodas. On poker night, he removes the coin on the string and makes us pay 40 cents," Daddy said.

I wasn't ready to go inside, so I climbed that large weeping bottlebrush tree that provided shade, with its long arms hanging open like an umbrella. The green and red fingers were the bristles where I often saw a bee buzzing. Despite a few stings, I loved climbing that tree and named it the "red bee tree".

I reached the second tier of branches and observed my neighbors. While some were mowing their lawns, others were busy picking vegetables or sneaking cigarettes in their garages. They were all unaware that I was observing them. The trend of watching the neighbors became something I enjoyed. It was the rumble of the old truck as it sputtered. It took my mind from drifting. Shannon and her parents pulled into the driveway next door.

"Are you going to Vivi's?" I overheard William ask.

I started down the tree but stopped when Shannon replied, "No, I'll stay home with you tonight." I felt disappointment come over me knowing that I would be home alone again.

Shannon was my best friend; I can't remember when we met because all my memories included her.

The sounds of Bob Seger's music awakened me. The earworm began

Old Time Rock & Roll blasting from Liv's bedroom ... *the kind of music that soothes the soul* ... Then, I realized, it's summer!

"Are you planning to eat something?" Mama asked as I shuffled to get my flip-flops on.

"No. I'm eating at Shannon's. She's making breakfast." I spun the bread loaf and placed the tie.

"You don't need to take all the bread for those fish," Mama yelled as I ran out of the house.

A short walk across the grass and through their chain-link fence to Shannon's house was where I found comfort. Her parents were young and fun. William and Wanda always had friends over and still took time to spend with us. They never locked their front door, and I never knocked.

"Good morning!" As I entered, it was the sizzle and smoky smells of bacon that caused my stomach to growl.

"You okay with scrambled eggs?" Shannon asked.

"Yeah, you know those are my favorite."

Shannon pushed the bread towards me. I pulled the heels from the loaf out of the bag and gave it a spin.

"We got four. That should be enough."

"What are you girls up to today?" William asked.

"We're going fishin' at Carmen's."

Together, we cleaned the dishes and prepared for our day on the lake. Summers on the lake kept us busy with swimming and fishing. We went to different spots depending on the time of day.

Shannon towed me on her bike while she peddled. I held the fishing poles, and the basket held the bread. A short bike ride to the end of Willowdale Road was where Carmen Ward and her family lived.

"You know I can't get those dirt worms on the hook. They move around too much," I said as she laid the bike down.

"You're afraid of the blood and guts that come out of the worm. That's why you should use the bread," Shannon said.

The Ward's had a small pug named Bruno who barked continuously as soon as we stepped onto the property. Mr. Ward would come out, and only he could keep Bruno quiet. He was yet another kind neighbor who spent time with us. On most days, Mr.

Ward would bring out his tackle and bait and throw a cast from the dock. He had fertile soil in his yard, and with good soil came good worms.

"Hey girls, how y'all been?" Mr. Ward asked.

We watched as he cast his line far into the lake, and in an instant, he was reeling one in. With a flick of his wrist, he pulled the hook out of the fish's mouth and returned the large bass to the water.

"Worms, all day, worms!" he proudly shouted. There was good money to be made with good fishing worms. The best ones were in his worm garden. "This lake doesn't have fish to eat, just fun to catch."

"We're gonna take the boat and check if that big bass is ready for us," Carmen said. She filled the cooler with cold drinks and snacks. She always had a Styrofoam cup of worms ready. We paddled to the dark spot, which seemed to hold all the fish. The problem was that only a boat could take you there. It was the high grass and Spanish moss that casts a shadow from below the old oak. It gave the dark spot its name. Supposedly, a four-foot alligator lived in the dark spot.

"Hopefully, the four-footer doesn't like bread. He could pull me in if I catch him."

"You're the same size," Shannon remarked.

I liked using bread. The first and last slices of the loaf were the best. I'd pinch off a piece, put it in my mouth, and get it wet and squishy. I threaded it on the end of my hook and hoped it stayed on while I cast my line. Carmen caught the first small bass, and with a knife, she'd cut it into pieces to use as bait. Not a minute passed, and she was reeling in a bigger one.

"Wow! That was awesome!"

Carmen wrapped the towel around the fish and released the hook from its mouth; gently, she placed it back into the water.

"Wait! Aren't you going to take it home? We can eat him," I said.

"Nah, these fish aren't for eating, just fun to catch," Carmen replied.

Shannon and I exchanged grins, as we knew it was time to go after only a few bites and nothing was caught. Besides, I was too busy keeping an eye out for the four-footer.

After a morning of fishing and a swim at the lake hole, we returned to Shannon's house for fried bologna sandwiches. The day was quiet as we swayed and napped in the hammock on that perfect summer day.

Before there were housing developments, deed restrictions, or Neighborhood Watch, there was Willowdale Road. I knew the names of everyone on my street, and they knew me.

Mr. Tim and his wife, Ms. Millie, moved in at the same time we did. I considered Mr. Tim to be one of my best friends. He was old, close to Daddy's age. Their trailer was close to the street, while the barn and garden were at the back of the property. The two spent their days in lawn chairs with umbrellas to cover them from the sun. Ms. Millie liked to cut up a watermelon for us to share and kept a pitcher of sweet tea always ready. Their dog Sissy and I would play fetch and roll around while they told their stories of living in Plant City on a strawberry farm. Mr. Tim liked to play riddles and games with me. Raising his hand and pointing to the sky, he asked, "If the sun rises east and sets west, where is north?"

He would show me how to prune the garden and pick the vegetables when they were ripe. We ate carrots from his garden after washing them off at the spigot. I enjoyed watching him work on his truck while he talked to me about school. He affectionately called me Little Bit, showering me with attention.

"Now, Little Bit, you listen here. It's important to stay bright and never give up on your learnings, ya hear?" Mr. Tim spoke with a twang and used slang compared to my teachers' words.

"Mr. Tim, I noticed you have old bikes in your barn."

He offered to let me have one if I helped him restore it. Although green was my favorite color, I chose the blue one because it had the least amount of rust. We removed the chain and banana seat, and together we spray-painted it blue again. A small loop of rope added to the handlebars allowed me to slide my fishing pole through. A weaved basket tied on the front to carry my bait. It was a great bike, and I rode it everywhere.

The Cates family lived next to Shannon. They had two sons, both older and off at college. Mr. Powell's house was across the street, and Mr. King's property was to his left. They both lived on the lake. The lakeside properties were larger than the others on Willowdale Road. Mr. King's house sat on the lake where the bend in the half-moon was. I always thought his name was fitting since it was the largest on our street.

Occasionally, when I climbed the red bee tree, I watched as he walked around on the top of his house. It was the only one with a rooftop sundeck, and I wondered if he could see all the way to Tampa from up there.

Half Moon Lake Road faced the back of our property. If you walked to the end, a path to the right led to the lake hole. A path to the left led to the Taylor's property. Cliff Taylor lived on Half Moon Lake Road, hidden by a driveway so long that his house and two trailers remained unseen. His parents had lived there until they both moved to a nursing home.

As much as I loved swimming in the lake, fishing, and riding my bike, summer had a dark side. Anyone from the outside would see that we had good parents and a lovely home. My dad went to work every day and provided well for our family. Years passed before all this changed. They would know he died, *but only I'd know I killed him.*

JUNE

My dad named me Vivian Rose. Vivian means *lively*, and Rose was derived from his first name, Rodas. It means *where the roses grow*.

"You are the lively rose that grows," he said. I was happy when Liv started calling me Vivi; it caught on with everyone in the neighborhood.

It was my birthday! Shannon asked if I wanted to go for breakfast with her and her parents.

Leaving the Waffle House, William asked, "How about a walk through the flea market? You girls go pick out a gift for Vivi's birthday."

I chose the badminton and volleyball set, and when we returned home, William helped us set it up. Mr. Tim was over with Mr. Powell, and the two watched us play. It was his recognizable whistle that caught my attention. He waved me over.

"Today's my birthday!" I announced.

"Happy Birthday, we got something here for ya," he pointed to the ground, where a pile of bamboo was tied together. Its green and yellow colors formed a pattern.

"What is it?"

"Well, it's a raft for you and your friends to go fishin' or paddle to the lake hole," Mr. Powell explained.

"It's pretty. I like the green stripes."

"Let's go down to the water and see how it floats. Go ahead, grab the line, and handle it yourself," Mr. Tim said.

And I did. I dragged it to the lake, kicked off my flip-flops, and threw myself onto it. It had two small paddles attached to it with a rope. One at the front right side, along with a soft cushion that was screwed into the bamboo, and the other at the back left side with another cushion. I sat there holding my paddle and imagined Shannon sitting up front, rowing along.

"You sit at the back when you're by yourself. Those loops, they're for ya to hang on to while you get yourself settled," Mr. Tim explained.

I was floating. It took me a while to get the hang of the paddle.

"YOU'LL NEED TO ALTERNATE YOUR ROWING," Mr. Powell shouted.

I struggled and found myself going in circles.

"Slow it down, one row left, one row right," Mr. Tim calmly offered.

I was getting it and was moving forward, but in the wrong direction. I realized that if I held the paddle in the water and pulled back, it could change my movement. They were smiling, no longer yelling.

As I moved closer to the dock, I said, "I got it. I can row it slowly, and it still moves forward. It's a fast mover."

"You'll have to give it a name. Every boat needs a name," Mr. Powell said.

"It's good that you're lightweight, since the bamboo is light."

"You think Carmen, Shannon, and you can use that together?"

"Oh yeah, we're gonna be all over this lake now."

I made it to the bank, holding the lead rope as I dragged it out of the water and onto the bank.

"The Green Machine! That's what I'll call it. This is the best birthday gift ever! Did y'all make this?"

"Yeah, we sure did," they said in unison.

They were proud of themselves and me. I dragged it to the driveway.

"You can leave it behind the shed if you'd like. It's closer to the water than your daddy's back barn," Mr. Powell suggested.

"I'm gonna show Mama and Daddy first, then bring it to your shed."

I walked inside to the sweet smell of something baking. "Mm, are those brownies?"

"No. It's a chocolate cake," Mama replied.

"Can you come out here? I want to show you what Mr. Tim and Mr. Powell made for me."

"Ay, mira que linda." She thought it was beautiful.

Daddy asked, "How much do they want for it?"

"Nothing. They made it as a gift." Pointing to the volleyball net, "Look what Shannon bought me for my birthday."

Daddy just walked back inside and shook his head. Sometimes, I wondered why he couldn't be happy. He would've been proud to show it off if it were his idea.

Mr. Powell was up early. "Mornin', Vivi. We're headin' out on the water today. Would you and Shannon like to tag along?"

"Sure! But first, Daddy wants me to pay you for the RC I've been drinking."

"Ah, all right. I'll add it to your credit. You keep coming over here and grabbin' a soda as much as you like. Tell your daddy if you don't come over to get a soda, who will I talk to?"

"Aw, Mr. Powell, you got Ms. Sherry to talk to."

"Yeah, but Ms. Sherry don't listen to my stories like you do."

"I'll be back, I'm gonna get Shannon."

Mr. Powell had a way of showing his kindness. It was the attention that I wasn't used to at home. Some of the best days on the lake were when he taught us to stand on water skis and zipped us around the lake in his speedboat. That's how he met his girlfriend, Sherry. They both used to work at Cypress Gardens as part of the famous waterski team. He told the same stories of the tricks he learned and the injuries he suffered. Only good memories of the men she met filled Sherry's mind. It was fun to watch them as they both flirted and laughed with each other.

When I got home, I shared my story and how we spent the day.

Daddy got up and walked away. "That old man doesn't need you riding in his boat and wasting his time," he said.

"He invited us and taught us to ski. I got up three times today and only fell six times, but we had fun."

"Vivian, you go ahead. Daddy is just mad that Mr. Powell took his money at poker and bought another boat. That's all," Mama replied.

Later that night, I wrote in my journal about my birthday.

How is it that the kindest men live right here in my neighborhood, and I got stuck with Daddy?

And don't tell Shannon, but 'The Green Machine' is my favorite gift!

SUMMER

The skies were soft blue with puffy white clouds, and the sun's heat felt like a burned kiss on my face. Florida was unbearably hot and sweaty every day in August. Only a few people could handle the heat. If you were driving south, you could feel the humidity like a warm, invisible blanket that settled on you as you crossed the Georgia-Florida line.

I've only known one person who liked the heat: my sister, Olivia Marie. Only Daddy and Mama called her Olivia. I called her Liv.

She always said, "The humidity keeps my curly hair calm." She was tough, and I had always admired her bravery. Liv once shouted at Daddy, asking him to stop yelling at Mama. He took a hand to her face.

"You shut your damn mouth and never raise your voice over mine," he said.

Despite her bleeding lip, she refused to back down, expecting another smack. But it didn't come.

Liv was tall and thin, with dark hair and soft brown eyes. She loved the sun; most days, she wore a bathing suit top, cut-off blue jean shorts, and flip-flops. Mama and Liv disagreed on two things: the way she dressed and how she always wanted to be out of the house.

"Ay Olivia, por qué causas tantos problemas?" Mama asked. Liv wanted to take the car to visit her friends; she knew walking would take too long. Mama hated telling her no, but Daddy would be angry if she allowed her.

"Why must you create so many problems? Why can't you stay

home and relax and enjoy the day here?" They argued.

She never wanted to stay home once she had a boyfriend. That was the actual reason Liv wanted to borrow the car. She and Billy started dating before he graduated from high school. He joined the military soon afterward. Daddy doesn't know yet. Mama had often told her, "Your secrets will cause many problems when your father finds out."

I was up having my morning cereal while the two continued. Mama thought I didn't know what she was saying, but I had learned to understand Spanish better than I could speak it. I knew Mama would give in and let her take the car. I called Shannon and Carmen.

"Come over soon; we can get a ride to the lake hole with Liv."

A few moments later, I took my shot with an innocent grin and asked, "Mama, can Liv drive Shannon, Carmen, and me to the lake hole today?"

And there, they both stopped arguing. Liv looked at me with a smile.

"I'll drive them to the lake and hang out with them. We'll only stay a few hours and come home before Daddy does. Is that okay?"

Mama knew we would not stop asking. She gave in. "Si, esta bien."

And we all gave a shout, "Woohoo!"

I learned to stay on Liv's good side. After we picked up Billy and arrived, we could see that the heat of summer had brought everyone out. The lake hole was at the topside of the half-moon. It was the only section that was cleared and offered a shallow beach. A big oak tree stood above the space where everyone gathered to swim. A pile of towels and flip-flops laid.

While Liv and her friends reunited, Shannon, Carmen, and I played a game of, 'How long can you hold your breath?'

Nearby was a group of older boys that Billy recognized. They began a game of their own. They formed a circle where one person was in the center, eyes closed, as he went under to grab a fistful of mud. Rising to the chants of "man out of water", they would sing, and he would throw the mud toward those singing. Those in the circle would dodge and jump away from being hit. I saw this was going to go badly when I swam out of the lake and sat near the tree to watch.

Liv and her friends stood nearby as one boy hurled a pile of mud, causing it to land right next to Carol with a *splash* and *kerplunk*.

"Hey! STOP IT!" she shouted.

Liv turned around and gave a warning, "If you hit one of us, I'm gonna make you eat that mud."

Before anyone realized what he was doing, the kid named Marco flung a handful of mud directly at Liv, and it smacked the side of her face.

"Liv, WATCH OUT!" I screamed, too late to warn her.

She went under and resurfaced like a snake as she slid across the water. They opened their circle, giving way for Liv to enter; Marco turned, splashing, but Liv still caught him. With a handful of his hair in one hand and mud in the other, she shoved the mud into his mouth.

"I told you not to throw mud at me!"

Everyone was staring at them. Marco was spitting and crying, embarrassed. In silence, we stood, and the water remained calm. Liv had everyone's attention as she returned to her circle of friends and continued talking.

"I told him. He should have listened."

On that day, Liv gained a reputation for herself. No one messed with her, which meant no one would talk to her. It created a reputation for me, too. When I went to the lake with my friends and saw Marco, they would whisper and stare. I'd stare back and give a face of, "Yep, don't mess with Liv's sister."

The property next to the lake hole was where the Kennedy boys spent their summers. Their grandma was Old Lady Kennedy; her property had a chain-link fence on both sides of her small cottage house. At the end of each fence line was a red ribbon tied to the poles. There were days when we played, splashing and making a commotion. Old Lady Kennedy would come stumbling out of her house with her arms flailing and fingers pointing. "You kids get out of my water! Stay off my property! Go on now! Git!"
We'd swim back to the hole and ask, "How can she own the water?"

There was a rumor that she would leave raw chicken on the bank of her property during the nights to allow the alligators to come and feast. That began the nickname "Gator Lady".

The last weeks of summer had arrived. I was awake before dawn and snuck out of our house. I ran and knocked on Shannon's bedroom window, and she opened the front door for me to enter. Sometimes we fell back to sleep and waited for the sun to rise.

During breakfast, I called Mama to tell her where I was. She always replied, "Mi imagino que ahí es donde estabas."

"Was your mom worried when you weren't home?" Shannon asked.

"No, she imagined that this was where I would be."

Shannon and I had a special bond, stronger than sisters. From the time we were young, there were secrets to come that she and I would share. She was a person of few words, making her perfect for keeping secrets. Strong, honest, great cook, and loyal friend—not one for long conversations. She was the person you always wanted by your side. I wanted to be like her someday. Fearless.

Most mornings, we packed a bag with sandwiches and bread for bait, grabbed a few cold ones from Mr. Powell's garage, and loaded our fishing gear onto The Green Machine. We learned that if we set sail from Mr. Powell's bank and floated toward the lake hole, we could see onto Mr. King's property.

"I'm determined to get on that sundeck one day. I'm eager to see the view from up there."

We saw Mr. King working in the yard, as he planted flowers and trimmed the bushes. We never saw his wife or children. But I heard he had a daughter living in Siesta Key.

"Stop waving to him. He doesn't like kids and he'll never let you on his property," Shannon said.

"I know. I'm going to kill 'im with kindness. If I wave enough times, he's bound to wave back. I'll get on that sundeck one day."

Shannon kept paddling as I dragged my line, making our way towards Carmen's dock.

YBOR CITY (EE-BOR)

Daddy's birth name was Rodas Perez, but he introduced himself as Rodie.

He was born in 1918 and raised in West Tampa near Ybor City. Daddy was always someone who did things on his own terms.

His father passed away when he was a teen. I wondered if his own father's absence was the reasoning behind his lawlessness. His mother, Juliette, remarried and made their home in West Tampa along the Hillsborough River. I once asked about his stepdad, and his reply was, "He will never be considered as my father."

His half-brothers never came to visit us, and their absence made me realize their strained relationship went deeper than he admitted.

There on the river was where Daddy grew up and recalled his stories of fishing and having a boat. I wondered if his childhood memories of living on the river are what brought me to love living near the lake.

It was during those times that we learned of what his life was like growing up in the 1930s. His mother, our Abuela Juliette, worked at the cigar factory in Ybor City.

Ybor was known as the largest cigar city since the 1800s. It held a fascinating history of hand-rolled cigars.

"Get up, get out, get under the sun!" Daddy sang.

"Wake up, we're going to Ybor today!" Liv said, pulling the blanket off of me.

I remembered going with Daddy to Ybor on Saturday mornings and walking inside the red and brown brick buildings that stood along its cobbled streets. We would go inside the factory to buy boxes of cigars, and then a short walk for some café con leche y pan con mantequilla at the Fourth of July Café. I sat on the café bar stool and watched as they made coffee using the silver cafeteira. Cuban coffee and Cuban bread with butter smothered across it only tasted so good because they would cut the bread in half and then cut it again at an angle. The triangular shape was the right size for dunking in a coffee mug. We drank strong coffee ever since we were young, and no adults objected; how the times would change.

We collected the week's groceries from the butcher, and groceria on our weekend trips to Ybor. The groceria offered candy and free samples of deli meats. Liv and I explored the boutiques, taking in the scents of cigars and Aqua de Violeta. While Daddy got a haircut at the barbershop, we savored our soft serve cones on a street bench. We watched the men and women, dressed in their weekend finest, scurrying up and down the streets.

There among us were the most common residents, as they shuffled and pecked along the brick road for crumbs. Ybor City's bird sanctuary offered a haven for the community's revered sacred chickens and roosters. The roosters and chickens called the dusty brick roads their home; we were just visitors.

South of Ybor was the Tampa Port, where Daddy later worked as a welder. He was married twice before he married Mama. When they eventually married, he was 24 years older than her and already had a son named Michael with his second wife. We hadn't yet met Michael, and Daddy seldom mentioned him. Daddy was tall and thin, with tanned skin that looked like wrinkled brown leather. He kept his hair slicked back, which had always been gray with speckles of black and short at the neckline. I couldn't imagine that he was ever young and handsome.

His work outfit was blue denim coveralls and black boots. On the weekends, he dressed in a white tank as an undershirt, dress pants, a belt, and black or brown wingtip dress shoes. I watched him as he chose the Guayabera from his closet. He loved his Latin-style button-up, collared dress shirts with vertical patterns and multiple pockets on the front.

But how I remember him most was wearing a plaid terry cloth bathrobe, with only a white tank underneath …

I've never been someone who enjoyed horror films. It goes back to my fear as a child. I realized that it's not the movie that scared me, it's the feeling of fear. In the movies, I'd watch the young girl as she awaited the killer to walk around the corner from the darkness. His shadow lingered in the doorway as he'd pause before coming at her; he'd stand near her, striking over and over. Out of fear, she couldn't scream. She couldn't move. She accepted the pain.
Or that moment when the shadow was hiding under the stairway, watching the victim take a step right in front of its outstretched hands.

My earliest memory of Rodas coming into my bedroom was when I was in preschool. It was the day of my first preschool photo; I was four years old. It was early in the morning when I heard Mama leaving for work and regretted not getting up. I fell back to sleep until I awoke with his hands on me. He touched me in places that he shouldn't have. I felt confused about what was happening. I avoided looking at his face, and I didn't want to hear the sounds that he made. I wanted to put my hands over my ears and push him away. None of it made sense.

When he was done with me, he walked over to the closet and picked out the blue dress with red polka dots. Mama made that dress for picture day. I was still sad when I arrived to meet the photographer, who placed me in my spot to take the fall photo.

He took his first snap. *Click.* "Why so sad? Come on, princess, let's show off that beautiful smile," the photographer said.

Mama bought the package of the smiling princess, and the photographer gave her the sad ones for free. He thought they were adorable, but inside my sad face, no one knew my secret.

Daddy's abuse would go on for years. The mornings were paralyzing. I held my breath so tightly that my chest heaved. Tears rolled down my face, and I wasn't even crying. Finally, with sweaty hands and my feet cramped, my bedroom door opened, and he stood there. As he walked toward me, I quickly closed my eyes to pretend I was asleep, hoping he wouldn't come in. But he did.

Those mornings before school transformed a fun and joyful young girl into a shy and insecure adult.

He comes for me.

Dear God, make him stop. I wish he were dead.

The Rooster's Arena

Daddy believed in keeping his friends close and his enemies closer. Some mornings, I walked with him to visit the neighbors. With a box of cigars, we headed to Mr. Tim's as our first stop.

"Tim, my friend. Let's enjoy a cigar!" Daddy spoke with a strong voice. The confidence in his tone made everyone like him and follow whatever he asked.

Wearing a large straw hat, Mr. Tim emerged from his garden of tall corn, his small frame hidden beneath his hat, like an umbrella pulled down too far.

There, Daddy pulled out two Cuban cigars. One he slid into Mr. Tim's shirt pocket, and the other he handed to him. Mr. Tim spat tobacco out of his mouth and he and Daddy bonded over a smoke. He knew the purpose behind Daddy's gesture of giving cigars to the neighbors. It was no secret; he wasn't shy about it.

"Are you plannin' on having friends visit today?" Mr. Tim wrapped the cigar through his arthritic fingers, pointing his cigar towards the back of the property. I stood there waiting while the two rambled on about things I had no interest in.

Mr. King's place was located directly opposite Mr. Tim's property. The wall of hedges was just above my head, but Daddy had a good view of spotting Mr. King. Proudly, Mr. King wore the creamsicle colors on a hat with a large brim that gave tribute to the Tampa Bay Buccaneers. As Mr. King rode along on his mower with a wave and a nod to Daddy, I watched as he placed two cigars on the gate to the driveway.

We walked on. Mr. Powell liked to sit in his garage and sneak a smoke of his cigarettes.

"You got a poker game tonight?" he asked.

"I'd like to have you over after 4:00," Daddy handed Mr. Powell one cigar.

I wondered why he only got one cigar, and the others were given two. But I knew better than to ask. My guess was that Daddy was still mad that Mr. Powell took the last lot on the lake. Mama shared the story, 'Your father wouldn't pay what Mr. Powell paid for that property.'

We headed back across the street to Shannon's place. William was in the yard, raking up pine needles.

"Hey there, Vivi. Shannon's inside if you want to go in."

I heard Daddy say to William, "Come by after 4:00."

Shannon was lying on the sofa watching television.

"What are you doing today?" I asked.

"Not much. I woke up with a headache and have been lazing around since. Was that your dad talking to mine?"

"Yeah, Daddy is having people over today after 4:00."

"So, he's passing out cigars?"

"Yeah, those cigars are like an invitation to his party."

It was 3:00 when Wanda let me know Mama had called, asking me to come back home. I knew I would work in the back barn tonight.

While returning to our yard, I could hear Daddy's activity in the barn. The music was playing from the back of the property. My hips couldn't resist swaying to Julio Iglesias' velvety voice singing *Guantanamera*. I walked inside, sashaying my shoulders and swaying my hips as I sang along to the Spanish words. I wasn't sure if I was singing the words correctly, but still I enjoyed singing in another language.

"Yo soy un hombre sincero, guajira Guantanamera..."

Mama stopped to watch me. She laughed and joined me with a few steps of her own.

Feeling embarrassed, I stopped dancing.

Hiding her smile, she smirked. "Go to the back. Your father is waiting."

Our property was over an acre. The front, where the house and carport sat, was a clean lawn with a few trees that provided shade. Mama had roses and hydrangeas across the front and a large gardenia bush in the corner. The left wall had a line of pink azaleas that peaked along the windowsill. A chain-link fence surrounded the entire back of the property. In the backyard beyond the gate, there were chicken-wire cages scattered throughout. Each cage held one to two hens, chickens, baby chicks, or a rooster. I learned early on that Daddy called them chickens if they could not lay eggs. They were hens if they did. Liv told me that the chickens were just a coverup for what was happening in the back barn.

On any other day, Daddy would be back there welding those iron rods together, the glow of fire and sparks bouncing off of his helmet and gloves.

Brap, brap, brap! The sounds were loud and screechy from the machine that powered his torch. We knew to stand a distance away while he worked. He transformed rods into stunning iron gates and window coverings, selling them to Ybor's boutiques and shops. His work could be spotted throughout the streets of West Tampa.

But once a month, on a weekend, Daddy would invite men he had met from South Tampa to the house. I don't think he referred to them as "friends" because he handled everything as a business. They would park their cars one behind the other next to the house and line both sides of the street. Men would come down the pathway dressed in their best weekend attire.

The back barn was a long semi-circle structure connected from the left side, along the back, to the right side of the property. Daddy built it before he ever built the house. Sunlight made the tin roof shimmer while wooden beams acted as pillars along the barn's right side. It was a covered stall and trough for the horse that Liv once had.

Daddy often was in the barn cleaning fish or crabs on those mornings he had been fishing on the Gandy Bridge. It was in the back barn he referred to as "his office". There, he had a refrigerator, countertop with a double hot plate, sink, RC Cola machines, a table, and chairs. It was here that he often played dominoes and poker with his friends. The scent of Cuban cigars hung in the air alongside the aroma of freshly brewed Cuban espresso.

There were ashtrays and matches scattered throughout, while the unlocked RC Cola machine provided free cold drinks for the evening. At the entrance, he had a private phone line and an old radio above the doorway. Hearing the music was how I knew he was back there.

Those nights when Mama needed him to come to the house for dinner, we would call his phone. We weren't allowed in his office unless he was there. Truth be told, I didn't enjoy being back there at all. It was dirty and dark. Hooks of long steel rods and various metal objects hung from the wood beams running along the walls. Various bicycles and rolls of chicken wire were mixed in with the cluttered assortment of welders' helmets and torches. A walkway was laid using boards along the dirty floor.

To the left of the office was an open space, and on the back wall was a line of six dirty white cabinets. A peg of wood with a nail below it held the cabinets shut. Scratch marks on the outside showed the peeled and flaked paint. And beyond that was where the *arena* stood.

The arena was a large circular structure; covering the dirty floor were sawdust and wood shavings. The lower wall panels were just below my eyes view, and above was a wall of chicken wire that connected the structure to the roof of metal and wood beams. Iron rods were used to strengthen the arena's walls. An old screen patio door was attached for Daddy to enter. Inside the circular space were two larger cabinets, built the same, side-by-side. The paint was gone, and the scratches were deeper. Two pegs and nails were on each door to hold the fighter inside. In the center of the arena, hanging from the roof beams, was a thick wooden dowel connected by stiff and heavy ropes. It hung there like an aerial trapeze pole, ready for its acrobats.

Liv was there to help Daddy keep track of the money exchanged, and I was there to keep the men happy with drinks and cigars. As soon as they entered the barn, Daddy would collect the fee, counting and shuffling the dollars and handing them to Liv. She would place the money in a zippered bag, and I would ask each one, "Would you like a drink?"

Daddy kept beers and Malta cold in the refrigerator. Most of the men wanted an espresso or an RC. But there was one guy named

Manolo who liked to drink beer and always brought his own. He spoke mainly in Spanish and looked at me and Liv with creepy eyes. I kept his beers coming until Liv told me, "Slow down on giving him beer; bring him a café, too."

Once the men had filled themselves with cigars and drinks, the chatter died down as Daddy instructed Liv to take the bag of money back to the house. We were told not to walk the pathway to the house, so we exited out the back of the barn where the gate was open. This was a sure way to avoid the risk of running into men still making their way. Mama and Liv would place the money bag inside the safe in Daddy's closet. Liv would return to help me with drinks and cigars. But then, Daddy would step inside the arena and yell for Liv and me to go, now! "Salir, ahora!"

The men continued their chatter, being as loud as the chickens and roosters amongst them.

Until the next day, when another group of men would come, and a new set of roosters would hide in the cabinets, awaiting their fate.

As I grew older, I discovered that most of the neighbors did not like Daddy's *monthly meetings*. Even though some of them didn't smoke cigars, they accepted cash bribes. I never realized what he was doing was illegal, and Mama later told us we moved to Carroll Pines so Daddy could have his arena.

Some people say that Daddy entertained members of the Tampa Mafia in our barn. But that secret was never told.

THE PACT

I welcomed the end of summer and looked forward to being back in school.

Each year on Halloween, Mr. King opened his gates. On this night, children of the neighborhood could follow the trail of old plastic pumpkins, filled with lit candles. This was my favorite house in the neighborhood.

The long driveway of dirt and white seashells led to a beautiful red and black brick house with black shutters and a front door to match. The large wraparound porch was white and welcoming, with wooden rocking chairs and beautiful fall flowered planters on either side of the door. His yard was immaculate, with freshly cut grass and wide pine trees that cast shade over the lawn—a hammock on one side of the property overlooked the lake.

As we approached the large double doors, we sang, "Trick-or-treat! Smell my feet …" It was the echo of our foot stomps that gave us away. Mr. King opened the door before we could finish our song. I stretched my neck, hoping to catch a glimpse inside, but he quickly closed the door. I wanted so badly to go inside and see. Mr. King only passed out Wrigley Spearmint gum packs.

He never said much except, "Don't y'all drop candy wrappings on my property."

"Catch you next year, Mr. King!" I shouted.

~

Shannon and I looked forward to the weekend. Saturday, after fishing, we rode bikes past the burned house to check if anyone was in "our place". The burned house was a small, abandoned shack, survived most of the fire from years ago. There we walked around inside and took shelter on rainy days. Next to the burned house was a dirt path that led past two run-down trailers. Tall grass grew on either side of the pathway that led to the back of the property where Cliff Taylor lived.

"Let's see how Cliff is doing," Shannon said.

Cliff was a tall, skinny man with a tan body and long, bleach-blond hair. Shannon's parents were friends with Cliff's family. From time to time, she would bring him food and pay him a visit. Shannon told me the stories of when her dad helped Cliff and his father build his house. They used plywood that was arranged vertically. The house appeared taller and had an entrance that was a hole in the wall shaped like a door, complete with hinges. Above the door was a cutout glass window in the shape of a crescent moon. There was no doorknob, just a looped rope and a bell beside it.

We rang the bell without an answer. Shannon pulled on the rope, and the door creaked open. It was dark as she stepped in.

"Cliff, you home?" Shannon called out. He didn't answer. We walked inside and immediately smelled a stench of rottenness. She walked over to a lamp and switched it on while I stayed in the doorway. There, lying on the sofa, was Cliff.

What I noticed first when the light hit his face was the color of his skin. He looked yellow, blue, a stale green. His face was sunken, and he was wearing only shorts, which made him appear skinnier than I remember. His arms and legs had scabbed sores and pink ones that were still raw.

"Hey Cliff, we dropped by to visit. Are you okay?" Shannon kept asking. "Have you taken your medicine today?"

Fear overcame me, and I could sense something was wrong. "I don't think he's breathing; he's not moving."

Shannon touched his foot. "Ooh! It's cold and stiff!" she moaned. Together, we rushed out of the house and shut the door. Concerned about an animal getting inside and eating his body, we placed a rock in front of the door to keep it closed.

We rushed to Shannon's, and curiosity overcame me, so I asked. "Ms. Wanda, do you know who lives in those trailers and that old house behind the burned house?"

"Cliff Taylor lives in the 'half-moon house', and those trailers are empty. His family owned that property, but I heard that his mother moved to a nursing home after his father passed away," Wanda said.

With eyebrows raised, we knew something was wrong when she told us that Cliff had leukemia, and she wondered if he had moved away as well. Shannon and I talked about telling Wanda what we had discovered. But afraid that we'd cause more trouble for Cliff if the police saw his indoor greenhouse and the many plants he grew, we decided not to.

Shannon said, "Those plants are illegal."

We planned to return the next day and check if he was still on the sofa or if he had regained consciousness from his medication and was alive. We didn't know what leukemia was, but it didn't sound good.

Part of the deal for me to stay overnight at Shannon's was I had to help with chores. In the morning, we cleaned, vacuumed, and dusted the tables. If William needed help with firewood, he'd chop it, and we'd throw it in the red wagon. I'd sit on the pile of wood as Shannon drove the wagon to the back of the property, and together we'd empty it for the night's bonfire.

We stopped for lunch and cut up a watermelon.

"Watermelon is sweetest on a hot day," William said.

Shannon reminded me, "We need to go check on Cliff." We cleaned up and asked if we could go ride bikes.

"Sure, don't be late, so we can start the fire together."

We slyly rode our bikes on a longer path to remain unnoticed. Half Moon Lake Road led to a hidden, shorter pathway to Cliff's place. I never told Shannon, but I knew Cliff because my sister talked about him. He was the older guy, in his 30s, who would get pot for Liv and her friends.

Riding up, we noticed the rock was still in place. Shannon slowly pulled the rope, opening the door that allowed the sunlight to creep in. We followed the beam of light to the sofa and still lying on top was Cliff. His foot was in the same position we had left it the day before. We didn't go inside; Shannon closed the door and put the rock in place. As we rode our bikes away, both of us were quiet. I wanted to cry, but no tears would come. I looked over at Shannon; she had tears rolling down her face.

"Don't you think we should tell someone about Cliff?" I asked.

"If we tell them we've known since yesterday, the police will accuse us," Shannon said.

We lived in the country where bonfires were how you got rid of your trash. Nights at Shannon's house were truly exciting. They had big rocks around the fire pit for us to sit on while we cooked hotdogs over the heat. Watching them bubble as they cooked gave me thoughts of Cliff. We roasted marshmallows on skewers and squashed them onto melting chocolate over a graham cracker. William and Wanda invited their friends, and we enjoyed singing to Bob Seger's music by the fire. Some nights, they'd put up tents, and we'd sleep under the stars. Shannon had the best parents, and we had the most fun together.

On that night, we became blood sisters for life with a piece of glass; we cut our palms until they bled. Shaking hands, we squeezed and mixed the blood to form a pact.

We agreed, "We will be blood sisters and keep our secrets for life."

Cliff was dead.

A few days passed, and I overheard Daddy's conversation with Mama. Ms. Millie and Mr. Tim had gone over to check on the Taylor boy the same day we were there. Mr. Tim had called the police, and an ambulance came to collect his body.

"I wonder why the ambulance had no sirens and lights on," Mama said.

"The boy is dead. No reason to rush," Daddy replied.

"Ms. Millie informed me that when they arrived to deliver his medication, they discovered him dead on the sofa. They found it suspicious that a rock blocked the door, and a lamp was toppled over. Cliff must have died in his sleep. It's better that he died in his sleep than to live with cancer," Mama said.

That was the day I learned the word cancer and understood it. It meant death. I told no one what we had seen, or that we had ever been to Cliff's house. Anytime anyone mentioned his name or the story, I acted as though I didn't know who he was.

Cliff? Who's Cliff? Where did he live? Nope, I don't know him.

That was the truth. I had never *actually met* Cliff.

Part Two

Goodbye

FREEDOM

Daddy always said, "You girls aren't leaving this house until your wedding night."
He made it clear that he was in charge of me, Liv, and Mama. With a twenty-four-year age gap, he could have been Mama's father. And he treated her like a child some days. When Mama started working at the sewing factory in Ybor City, he was not happy.

"You want to tell the neighbors and your friends at work that your husband can't afford to take care of his family? This is my house. I make the money, and I spend it," Daddy yelled.

Mama just looked down and hoped he did not hit her. But not Liv. She watched them argue.

"Please don't say anything, Liv," I begged.
But Liv never listened to anyone.

"Don't treat Mama like that," she snapped back.

"You are girls who will become just women, and women have no role in this world except to be alongside a man. Know and learn your place!" he shouted.

I couldn't move from my hiding spot on the couch, hoping the pillows would shield me from the vibration of his voice. Once he left the room, I ran to hide in mine. In the morning, we pretended as though nothing had ever happened. Until next time.

So, when the school report cards arrived, they discovered Liv had not passed. She had multiple absences and failed classes and would have to repeat 11th grade.

"I refuse to let my teenage daughter embarrass me by living on the streets," Daddy said.

Liv threatened to move out and live with her boyfriend. That night, Liv snuck out of her bedroom window, and Billy picked her up. She left a note on her bed explaining that she would stay at Billy's mother's house and call soon. After two days had passed, the phone rang.

"When's a good time to get more clothes?" Liv asked.

"Your father and I have been worried sick these past few days. We don't know where Billy's mother lives or if you are safe. Now you call to ask for more clothes?" Mama said.

"No, I also called to let you know I plan to live with Billy's mom."

I had never witnessed Mama screaming at Liv the way she was. Her voice became so loud. She knew they were losing Liv, and her teenage years were gone.

"If you're so brave and ready to live like an adult, then you and Billy come here and speak to your father yourself!" She banged the phone into its carriage, without saying goodbye.

Billy graduated from high school at age 18 and joined the Army. He had finished his basic training and would leave for Arizona in April. I had overheard Liv and Billy discussing their plans to live together, but I never told Mama. Now, listening to Mama and Daddy argue made me realize this would get worse.

"She wants to move with him to Arizona. If we keep her here, she'll continue to sneak out and run. If it's not this boy, it will be the next one."

He knew Mama was right. He knew Liv would do as she pleased, regardless of his approval.

"She is only a teenager with a child's mindset. She lacks the ability to make mature decisions," he said.

I was setting the table just before dinner when Daddy noticed I had set five plates.

"Who else is eating here?"

The front door opened, and Billy and Liv walked inside before I could respond. Liv acted as though nothing had happened.

"Hey Daddy, hey Vivi!" she said.

With a mere wave of his hand, Billy said very little. Carrying a tray of chicken and rice from the kitchen, Mama handed it to Daddy, and surprisingly, he said nothing when they both walked in.

Daddy sat down at the head of the table and placed his napkin. I followed his lead and sat in my chair next to his. Thankful that my seat was against the wall, I had a clear view of what could happen. Liv and Billy were gathering clothes in her bedroom, and you could hear the shift of things being moved around. Feeling a little panicked, I kept busy and passed the bread to Daddy while I kept my eyes on Mama as she moved back and forth to the kitchen.

"Olivia, hora de comer," Mama said.

Daddy repeated, knowing that Billy didn't understand Spanish. "Olivia, it's time to eat!"

The two sat across from me, and Mama sat at the end of the table. My eyes darted back and forth as the conversation continued. It made me nervous for both of them and, unfortunately, poor Billy was completely unaware of what was coming his way. I wasn't sure which would be worse for him to see, Olivia or Daddy.

This was Billy's first time meeting our dad, and Mama had only seen him out the window on those nights when Liv's friends came to pick her up.

Billy had dressed nicely, wearing a button-up shirt tucked in his jeans and boots. He had military-short hair, and Mama would say his deep blue eyes reminded her of Elvis. She liked Billy a lot, but wished Liv was not so young.

Mama passed the plantains and said, "Billy, it is good to finally meet you, and we are happy to have you for dinner."

Dabbing my bread into the black beans, I kept my eyes moving back and forth from Liv to Daddy. I wasn't sure how the two were staying so quiet. Had I known they would both be on their best behavior, I would have invited friends for dinner sooner.

Mama passed the tray of chicken and rice to Billy, and I noticed he had served the first plate that he passed to Liv. Then he served his plate and passed the tray to me. I looked up at him, and his blue eyes smiled at me. I saw kindness.

Daddy asked Billy about his job and how long he planned to serve in the Army.

His voice had a deep timbre, like that of an older gentleman, yet he spoke gently. Daddy took a second look at him when he noticed

Billy's soft tone. He looked directly at Daddy.

Yes, eye contact, that's good.

Daddy wasn't used to someone who faced him eye to eye.

And then the quiet calm was gone.

Liv spoke. "We decided I would continue living at Billy's house until April. Billy's mom said it's fine for me to stay with her. This works perfectly."

"What happens in April?" Daddy asked.

"Billy goes to Arizona, and I'll be old enough to go, too."

"Olivia, once you turn 18, you can do whatever you want and not ask anyone for permission, but you will only turn 17," Mama reminded her.

Oh boy. There it was. I leaned in for another piece of bread, grabbed my drink, and sipped, knowing that a table flip could happen at any time.

Daddy was quiet and continued to listen to their side. He glanced at Mama, and she raised her eyebrows.

And then Daddy looked at me. Keeping my eyes down, I felt his stare and scooped the rice into my mouth. His voice was elevated, but not yet at the point of yelling. He asked me, "Do you have an opinion on my teenage daughter's plans?"

I continued chewing and looked over at Mama.

And then he told us all.

"This is what we are doing. If you leave this house to live with another man, you will get married. Since you continue skipping your classes, it would be best to withdraw from school. You will stay living here until the wedding. If you live in this house and do not sneak out, I will go to the school and sign the papers for you to withdraw," he said.

Daddy looked at Billy and asked, "Billy, are you ready to be her husband and take care of her?"

His voice was shaky as he wiped his mouth with his napkin. He stuttered, "Yeah, yes, I love her and want to always be with her. I understand she is only 16, but she'll be 17 soon. If I were going to be living here, I'd wait for her. I would properly propose, be engaged for a year, and plan a wedding. But, when I joined the military, I was thinking about myself. I was thinking about my future. Even though

I was friends with Olivia then, I didn't know we would fall in love. The military can move me around the country at any time, and I could miss having the most amazing girl in my life all because of one year." Billy nodded. "Yes, we will get married. Liv can stay here until we can go to the courthouse and make it official."

Daddy's surprise was apparent, with his mouth open and his face drained of color. Billy kneeled on one knee.

"I didn't plan to do this tonight, so I don't have a ring. Olivia Marie, will you be my wife?"

Mama, Liv, and I had tears in our eyes. I blinked, and the tears streamed down my face. Liv was smiling. She stood and began bouncing around. Excited that she could quit school but not happy that she had to stay home.

"YES, I want to be your wife!" she shouted.

Standing, Daddy slammed his hand on the table. "Okay then, we plan a wedding!"

We began shopping for the dress. Liv wanted a long gown, and Mama said no to white.

"You can wear ivory," Mama said.

The long dress covered her feet. She tip-toed to take up the slack on each dress she tried on.

"Is this long enough for me to wear high heels?" Liv wondered.

"Shouldn't a wedding dress have a long train?" I asked.

She lifted the dress, twisting herself to glance at her butt in the mirror.

"If we had more time, I'd get a longer gown."

When we got home, she put the dress on again to show Daddy. Mama bought a veil, but it was not intended to cover her face. Instead, it was a headpiece with long lace that fell down her back and extended to the floor.

"I never expected to see you in white lace," Daddy said.

I explained to Daddy what I had learned from our day of shopping.

"It's not white, it's ivory, and the lace is to add texture to her boobs. She can't wear white; she's not pure," I said.

"Shut up! What do you know about wedding dresses?"

Mama and Daddy laughed.

That night I wrote in my journal. *I will wear black when I get married. Then Mama won't need to tell me the rules of being pure.*

∽

Mama let her borrow a flower clip as they pulled her hair up in a braided bun. Ms. Wanda and Ms. Jones came over early and helped her look like a bride.

"It is important to not look like someone we don't recognize on your wedding day. A touch of makeup and beautiful hair will bring a bridal look to your photos." Ms. Jones dabbed her cheeks with color.

"I was hoping for dark makeup on my eyes," Liv said.

Mama reminded her that today was special and asked her not to argue. Liv's anxiety was apparent. As her legs shook, she continued smoking, using one cigarette to light the next.

"Why am I so nervous? Should I be this nervous?"

"Don't be nervous; it's just Billy and a few people from the neighborhood. You spend time with these people every day," I reminded her.

"You're right." She exhaled. "Now, let's hope I don't fall in these heels!"

My hair laid with waves of curls down my back and baby's breath pinned like a crown.

For the wedding, Mama didn't have time to make me a dress. I had never owned a new store-bought dress. Normally, my dresses didn't have tags sewn inside them that displayed the size; if you looked closely, you could see the stitching that showed Mama handmade my clothes. That had always bothered me.

It was a long, soft pink rayon with pearly buttons down the sleeves, along with the white sandals that we had bought for this day. And I had to admit, in this store-bought dress, I looked amazing!

Mama arranged yard flowers into a beautiful bouquet—even making one for me to carry. The powder blue hydrangeas and white gardenias set against her dress gave Liv an elegant look.

All of Billy's family and friends attended the wedding. Mr. Tim and Ms. Millie brought potato salad and devilled eggs. Shannon and

40

her parents brought a covered dish, and Mr. and Mrs. Cates arrived just before Mr. Powell with his girlfriend, Sherry. Our house had never seen such a crowd.

"Will it still count if it's not in a church but at our house?" I wondered.

It was Liv's 17th birthday as Daddy walked her down the hallway in our house. Liv and Daddy walked from her bedroom to the living room, where the minister was waiting to greet them. As she walked, the scent of gardenias filled the air, enhancing the ambiance.

There were tables and chairs set up in the front yard, along with Cuban-style food that Mama had been cooking for two days. We had white rice, black beans, red beans with pork, yellow rice, and chicken, plantains, yucca, bread, and along the table were fat round bottles of red wine.

Daddy raised a glass and toasted. "This wine is cheap enough for a wedding! SALUD!"

After the meal, Daddy connected speakers to hear the sounds from Liv's record player inside and out. The music of *Can't Help Falling in Love* by Elvis played while Liv and Billy swayed to their first dance as a married couple. It was a grand party.

At the end of the night, we collected the rice-filled bags, then stood outside and tossed them overhead; Billy and Liv drove off in Liv's Volkswagen Beetle that Daddy had bought her. Liv was a married woman. Her name became Olivia Marie Miller. I didn't like it, and I still called her Liv Perez.

Their honeymoon consisted of driving to Arizona over the next two days. Billy had a week off from work before returning to the Army and their Happily Ever After began.

Once she and Billy were gone, I played the records she left and tried on the clothes I found in her closet. After rummaging through a few boxes, I found a bag with skinny cigarettes I gave to Mama. Later, I watched her flush them down the toilet. They must not have been the brand Mama smoked.

SOFIA

A framed photo sat on Mama's dresser in their bedroom. It was old and faded with dents on the once-sharp corners. I enjoyed the different stories that Mama would share each time I held that photo and asked, "Who is in this picture?"

Mama was born Sofia Ines Garcia. It was the name her mother gave her. There she stood, just days before her flight to Florida. She was tall and slender, with long, wavy, black hair that fell down her back and away from her face. Her thin jaw and highlighted cheeks revealed a slight glimmer that gave her a Hollywood smile. You could see the love and attention she gave to her mother as the two embraced, one arm behind each other.

Her dress impressed me, knowing she had sewn it herself. She told the story of how she struggled with the silk fabric but was determined to complete the dress. The bodice was dark silk taffeta, with a V-neckline and three-quarter sleeves, while the skirt was striped. It was difficult to tell the exact color from the sepia photo, dated 1965. I knew she was wearing high heels by the way she towered six inches over her mother.

Mama always called our grandmother, Abuela Mema. As the two stood facing the camera, Abuela Mema was wearing a white blouse and a gray skirt. But what I noticed most was the long gold medallion hanging around her neck. I only recognized it because Mama had worn it as long as I could remember. They took that photo days before she moved to Florida. She was 23 when she packed everything she could and moved to Tampa.

As a teenager, Mama had gone with her family to Tampa on

vacations. She told us stories of taking trips to Tampa, comparing it to other family trips to Cancun or the Bahamas. Having family and friends to stay with in Tampa made the trip easier.

I listened to Mama as she shared the story of her first flight, she spoke in a tone that showcased her Hispanic accent. Her English was very clear and still she over-pronounced each word.

"My first time in Tampa was when I was 13. My brothers and I flew with our mother on vacation to stay with her friend, Zoila. They lived on the west side, along the Hillsborough River. They had a beautiful house. She and her husband, Vincent, had two children of their own. Sylvia was two years younger than me. Her brother Orlando was 15."

Mama stopped for a sip of water and pulled a tissue from her pocket.

She continued, "Sylvia and her brother were in the local baseball league, and on that Saturday, they had team photos scheduled before the game. We had planned to meet them. Zoila drove Abuela Mema, myself, and my brothers to the park. We were stuck in traffic for a long time, and we didn't want to miss the start of the game. Zoila turned around and drove back-roads to the park. Once we arrived and sat on the bleachers, we looked around for Vincent, Sylvia, and Orlando. Zoila was confused and wondered where they could be. 'This is where they usually sit.'

"My brothers and I walked around the park to check if they had moved to a different field. Returning to the bleachers, we found Zoila and Abuela Mema crying.

One of the player's parents had told Zoila that there had been an accident, which was why traffic was so backed up. It was Vincent's car that had been in the accident. We quickly headed to the site where the accident had taken place. They had removed the vehicles, but Orlando remained on the roadside. Zoila reached him as the paramedics attended to the cuts on his face. He told Zoila they had taken Vincent and Sylvia to the hospital. When we arrived, we were told that Vincent and Sylvia had not survived the accident. Vincent was in a rush to get to the park, speeding and maneuvering through traffic, when a large car carrier flipped on top of their vehicle.

It was years later; I was visiting Zoila for Orlando's wedding.

He got married and had children of his own. Zoila remarried a man named Pablo, and it was there, on the Hillsborough River, that I met your father," Mama continued. "When I moved from Matanzas, Cuba, to Tampa, I stayed with Zoila until your father and I were married later that year. It was 1965, the last time I was in Cuba and the last time I saw my mother and brothers.

Initially, I had hoped my mother would come to Tampa for my wedding and Olivia's birth, but it became challenging to return to Cuba. I never went back to my country," she cried.

As the gold medallion hung from her neck, I watched as she rubbed it with memories of her mother.

VACATION IN THE DESERT

Mama and I needed some time to adjust after Liv moved to Arizona.

"I didn't realize how much your sister helped me around the house until now," Mama said.

"I didn't realize how much work I would have to do until now."

After cleaning the house, we had time to play games and listen to her music. Mama taught me to dance and move my hips to salsa. She stood behind me, gripping my hips, and smoothly guided them to move in rhythm. We laughed so hard and found ourselves missing Liv more. I helped in the kitchen, and Mama helped me with homework.

Mama made a chocolate cake with chocolate icing that year for my birthday. I called Liv, and holding the phone, I could hear her sing along as the two serenaded me, Happy Birthday.

The Fourth of July was always an enjoyable time in Tampa. Each year, the sewing factory where Mama worked had an annual company picnic at the local park.

"Which do you want, a Cuban or chicken salad sandwich?" Mama asked as she filled out the lunch card.

"Duh! Nothing beats a Cuban sandwich."

I overheard Mama talking to Liv on the phone that morning. She was upset that she was so far away and would be missing the company picnic.

I always enjoyed the kids' obstacle course, and Daddy played softball with the adults. Mama sat at the picnic table with a few of the ladies. She introduced me to all her coworkers again, although I remembered meeting them last year. Every year, they gossiped about the same people. I teased Mama that she was a part of her own Telenovela. And in the darkness, we enjoyed the fireworks.

A year after Liv and Billy got married, we noticed Liv calling more frequently, and she seemed sad and lonely.

Daddy talked to her first, passed the phone to Mama, and then to me.

"I miss you all so much, and Daddy says y'all may come to visit me."

The following week, we were on a family vacation to Arizona! It took Mama two days to pack and prepare the car for the road trip. She had packed everything she needed to cook at Liv's house. Mama's craziest plan was to bring fresh crabs to Arizona, and Daddy agreed. I could tell this would go poorly. *Who takes fresh crab in a Styrofoam cooler from Florida to the desert of Arizona?*

Our drive to Tucson was long, but it was nice when we stayed in a hotel after a full day of driving. It was my first time staying at the Holiday Inn.

We made it—and the crabs did too! My favorite part of the entire trip was that kids ate for free at the Holiday Inn, and they offered soft serve ice cream!

Liv joined us for breakfast at the hotel in the morning, and later that evening, we all went to Liv and Billy's apartment. Mama cooked crab and made chilau in her big metal pot. We visited the nearby park and had a picnic for Liv. She loved having us there with her, and I loved having the four of us together.

We went hiking up the hill that had painted rocks on it. The painted rocks formed the logo for the battalion Billy was part of. We took a drive around the base where he worked. I enjoyed seeing all the soldiers in their uniforms. They all looked the same and seemed so serious. No one was smiling. I wondered if they needed to focus or if someone had trained them not to smile while marching. I realized that was the difference between a civilian and a soldier. Soldiers take their job seriously; they are fighting for their country. Civilians are fighting for a paycheck.

The soldier leading the others would carry the American flag. Another soldier would march beside the group while he shouted out different cadences for them to repeat. They seemed to be hurrying and running everywhere they went. Most were rushing to the portable buildings.

"What is going on in that portable?" I asked. Back home, our school had portable classrooms. Maybe the soldiers were in class, learning songs and how to march in sync.

"I like the Army. I find it interesting how organized they are. Maybe I'll join when I'm older," I said.

"The hell you will. My daughters are not joining the military. They will send you to war just like the men." Daddy changed the subject. "Take in these sights, you won't see this back home."

To me, the view was the same, cacti and rocks, but to Mama, everything was beautiful.

"Ay, mira que linda!"

After two days of driving around the Fort Huachuca mountains and seeing all we could of Tucson, we stopped at a gas station.

"How long does driving to the Grand Canyon take?" Daddy asked.

Six hours later, we checked into a Holiday Inn near Grand Canyon Park. Liv came with us while Billy stayed at their house to work. It was nice having her around; it felt like we were a family again.

"I love Billy and being here with him, but it is difficult to find a job being so young. I get bored, and it causes us to fight a lot," she said.

"Do you want to come home with us?" Mama asked.

"No. I want to make it here. Billy thinks it'll get easier once I find a job and keep busy."

The following day, we awoke to a view of the most spectacular sights I had ever seen. From our hotel, you could see the mountain range. They transitioned from tall mountain peaks that floated above the clouds. The height and colors were towering and vibrant, with large rocks intertwined within the tall green trees. I imagined how it must appear from high in the sky. And still, I expected a canyon to look different.

"I was expecting more," I said.

"Oh, we are not there yet," Daddy replied.

We parked and walked around a few buildings that housed the gift shop and restaurants, and as we walked toward the edge, I stopped. The canyon was not what I had imagined. Miles of emptiness stretched in every direction below. The canyon reminded me of an image of God's fingers dragged along the ground, causing cuts in the earth left behind. It indeed was beautiful in its grandeur. We just stood there. All of us were watching, no one speaking. Mama continued taking pictures with her Polaroid.

"How did the canyon get here?"

"The mountain opened up when the river ran through it," Daddy said.

That was it?

He summed up this enormous canyon in one sentence.

"When I get home, I plan to check out a book on the Grand Canyon from the library. I need more detailed information."

I saw rich colors, in shades of brown, gold, and orange, and traces of blue and green in areas where the walls had been cut. The canyon was an emptiness below us, with only sections of fencing to hold us back from falling. No photo could do it justice.

After a few days of visiting the canyon, we drove back to Liv and Billy's place, ate lunch, and packed for home. Daddy left some money on their table, and we began our drive through the night. I fell asleep listening to Mama and Daddy discussing how glad they were that Liv did not want to return with us. She was making her marriage work, even though she realized 17 was too young and more challenging than she'd expected.

The wheels screeched as Daddy slammed on the brakes. I rolled from the backseat to the floorboard. As I lifted my head over the seat, I saw the deer, dead in the road. No other cars were on the highway at that hour. Even with a broken headlight and damaged bumper, Daddy insisted we kept driving until we saw the green "H" on the highway.

The following morning, as we left the Holiday Inn, I noticed Mama had added new towels and pillows to our home collection.

We finally arrived. That was the worst part of taking a vacation—the drive home.

That explained why rich people chose to fly.

It was a few months before Liv called again. She and Billy were getting divorced, and she needed to ship her clothes in a box to our house. Billy sold her car, which Daddy had bought when they got married. He told her he could not afford to pay for the divorce and for her flight to come home.

"I should have given you the money, not left it for Billy. You should have kept the car, thrown everything you could fit inside, and driven it home. I can give you the money to stay at the Holiday Inn, and if he wants to divorce you, he can figure out how to pay for that himself," Daddy yelled.

She snapped back, "Too late! He already sold it, and besides, I'm the one who wants the divorce!"

She was shouting at Daddy, knowing he could not smack her over the phone. I sat there listening, and I was proud of her. She wasn't afraid to stand up to anyone.

I knew I could never talk back to him, but watching how they communicated gave me hope he would one day show me this type of respect.

WINTER IN FLORIDA

Mama entered my room while I was listening to Liv's favorite album, Eagles' *Hotel California*. She turned the record player off and said she had to talk with me. She said it so fast that I wasn't sure if I heard her correctly.

"Daddy has been diagnosed with cancer. Do you know what that means?" Mama asked.

I lied. "No. Is it bad?"

The word cancer was something I had heard before and knew what that meant. My mind flashed back to the image of Cliff, *seeing his body lying there on the sofa, dead.*

"Daddy will need to go to the hospital for surgery, and you'll be staying with Ms. Millie and Mr. Tim on school nights this week. The hospital can take care of him, and he can get the medication he needs to feel better," Mama said.

That was when I realized the difference between Cliff's and Daddy's cancer. He would have lived longer if he had his parents or a wife to help him go to the doctor. But I knew Daddy would die. I knew because I prayed for this.

Liv returned home just before the holidays. There was a difference in her, a calmer and gentler person; she enjoyed spending time at the house on weekends and helped Mama take care of Daddy.

In the living room, she played her records for us to listen to. I had hoped that she had changed after getting married and moving far away. But I had a feeling she was acting the part of a "guilty daughter". Watching our dad deteriorate and seeing him weaken, I wondered if they knew something they weren't telling me.

On Christmas Eve morning, I received a phone call from Shannon.

"Some guys from the neighborhood have a Christmas gift for everyone. We should meet at the lake hole around eleven this morning," she said.

I told Liv about the Christmas gift at the lake from the guys. She was good friends with all of them and knew nothing about it. I went next door and got Shannon.

"Liv is going to drive us to the lake hole. She wants to go there early and find out what it is."

When we arrived at the lake, the Kennedy boys, and their dad were there. He was standing at the top of a ladder. "Don't let go until I'm on the branch," he said.

Mr. Kennedy was the first person to test the rope swing. Dressed in a tee shirt and jeans, he pulled himself onto the rope and sat on the tire like a swing. The boys pulled the rope back as he swung farther over the lake, stretched his arms, and fell backward into the water. Seconds later, he sprung out of the water.

"Woohoo! That was awesome! The water is cold, but it feels great! Who's next?" he shouted.

Each of us lined up, taking turns swinging on the rope. Initially nervous, I sat on the tire while they pulled it back and let it go.

"Let go! Let go, Vivi!" they shouted.

I swung out once more, but I released my grip that time! It was hard to see where I would end up as I fell backward. The cool water pulled me deep under, and swimming to the surface was invigorating. I had never swum out that far before.

We heard a crack as I got out of the lake to get in line for another shot of adrenaline. Alex was standing on the tire, bouncing as it went out over the lake. The large branch cracked, and the tree limb fell, dropping Alex into the lake near the shore. He landed on his back. His dad was there to see that he was fine. "Get up, Alex. You broke the tree," he laughed. And in return, we all laughed too.

There were no other branches that they could reach with the ladder.

"Merry Christmas. I'm glad you all could enjoy the gift once," Mr. Kennedy said.

On that cold Christmas Eve morning, we shared a gift of fun and fearsome adventure.

When people asked, "Do you swim in the lake all year?"

I always replied, "Of course, this is Florida."

Happy Valentine's Day!

After having waited too long to go to the doctor, the disease spread beyond Daddy's pancreas. Surgery failed to fully remove the cancer; medication only eased the pain. The doctor had given him six months to live from November. I got home from school and saw that he was not looking good. The sofa was his bed. His eyes looked tired, and his face was thin and pale. Where he towered over me before, his body now slumped and shuffled. I watched this beast change, as he was not the same man he was.

I had been working on my Valentine's cards all week. Mrs. Pardon gave us a list of everyone in the class.

I asked Daddy, "Can you help me tape a lollipop to each card?"

He held out his hand as I gave him the candy box. Lifting them one by one, I signed my name and a heart on each card. I felt confident in my cursive writing as I addressed each envelope with my classmate's name.

"Tomorrow is Valentine's Day, Daddy. I have some extra cards. Can I make one out to you?"

He did not respond, and I noticed he had fallen back to sleep. I found one with a rooster on the front and signed my name with a heart. On the envelope, I wrote in my best cursive, "Rodas, my Daddy," and left it there beside him.

The following morning, I saw Daddy and Mama sitting on the sofa sipping coffee.

"Daddy, you look better this morning," I said.

"I want you to come home after school and stay inside the house. I will be home when you get off the bus. And Daddy's son, Michael, is coming over later to visit with him. He may stay and have dinner with us, too," Mama said.

"Sounds good," I said as I headed out the door for the mile walk to the bus stop.

After exchanging valentines at school, I was glad I had an extra card for the bus driver. She also had a Valentine card for me. I was surprised when I jumped off the bus and saw Mama's car awaiting me.

Shannon and Carmen took a ride as well.

"Carmen, I can take you to our house. You'll have to walk from there," Liv said.

"I appreciate you driving to pick us up. The Valentine's party was amazing, and I have lots to carry," I said, getting in the car.

I noticed Liv did not look happy.

"Daddy has not been well today. He doesn't want to go back to the hospital, so Mama is with him at home," she said.

"Yeah, I know Mama told me that Michael is coming today to see Daddy," I reminded her.

Liv filled me in. "No, he called and said he could not make it today. But this weekend he may."

The mood in the house had changed. There was no music playing in the background, the television was on low volume, and for dinner, Mama was cooking chicken and rice soup.

The table that was decorated with fresh flowers and candlesticks was now covered with medicine bottles and a pitcher of water nearby. It was disturbing to see him asleep on the sofa. With a thin face, his cheekbones stood out, and his eyes seemed sunken. The sound of his slow panting and steady breaths made it hard to be near him.

While I was in my room changing out of my school clothes, I overheard Mama whispering to Liv, "He doesn't want to go back to the hospital. He wants to die at home."

I stayed inside with Liv and Mama to help when Daddy woke up and needed more water for his medication. Feeling hot and cold, he would signal by raising his arm to cue me to place the blanket. He would lift his leg when he was too warm. Mama gave him sleeping pills at night to help him settle down and get some rest. She told me I could sleep on the other sofa beside him and let her know if he stirred.

That night, Mama entered the living room and found Daddy gasping for breath. I awoke to the red lights flashing against the wall and the commotion over Daddy. It happened too fast to say goodbye. As Mr. Tim carried me to his house, I looked over his shoulder and saw the paramedics placing Daddy in the ambulance.

"You're gonna have a sleepover at my house tonight, Little Bit," he said.

In the morning, it took me a moment to remember where I was. I looked out the window and saw my house across the grass. The hallway was dark as I walked into the kitchen where Mr. Tim and Ms. Millie sat waiting for me to share breakfast.

"Little Bit, you want me to walk you over to the house when you're done eating?" Mr. Tim asked.

"No. I'll be fine, and Mama should be home."

When I walked inside, I overheard Mama on the telephone talking in Spanish about flowers and Daddy's brown suit. When she was off the phone, she and I sat on the sofa as she tried to explain.

"Daddy's not here. He passed away last night," she said.

Her eyes were wet and swollen, and she looked so sad. I hugged her. Liv was in her bedroom, still asleep. She had stayed with Mama at the hospital all night. There were no pills on the table, and the bed sheets were gone from the couch where Daddy had slept for the past months. I lay down, and the realization hit me.

It was not a dream. God heard my prayer. Daddy was dead.

To love someone and to hate someone. How would I ever understand that both feelings can exist simultaneously? Since then, Valentine's Day has never been the same.

A few days later, we went to the funeral. I wore a navy-blue plaid dress with a white scalloped collar. It opened when I twirled. Because this was a special occasion, I could wear my church shoes, shiny black patent leather with a gold buckle, and white ruffled socks. I brushed my long, dark hair and secured my bangs with a blue barrette.

You would have thought we were having another wedding with everyone from the neighborhood in their best dress. Liv told me it was a sad day, so I acted sad.

I noticed no one looked Mama in the eyes, and everyone had their head down.

I was unsure how to feel about *my loss*. Everyone kept saying that to me. What does that mean? When we arrived at the funeral home, we stood at the doorway and greeted each person as they came in.

"Oh, Vivian, I am so sorry for your loss," they kept repeating, leaning and hugging me.

At the cemetery, where we stood as Daddy's casket floated above the hole in the ground, I noticed a baseball field across the street. I pointed, "Well, at least he can watch baseball from here."

A few laughed. Liv stood beside me, nudging me with her arm. "These are Daddy's brothers—Uncles Phillip and Robert."

Reaching out my hand, I saw the familiarity in them both. With my hand still out to the young man that followed, I looked up and saw the hazel eyes that we shared. He was younger than I expected, and I needed no introduction.

"You're Michael, my brother?"

He nodded and said, "You're Vivian?"

"Yeah, and this is … *our* sister, Liv."

Still holding his hand, I pulled him beside me and said, "Stand here with us. He was your dad, too."

We stood beside one another as the line of Daddy's friends continued to arrive.

Someone handed me a card with a picture of Daddy on one side and a prayer on the other. The picture was old and faded. Daddy looked young, with black hair and youthful eyes. He was standing beside a giant-mouth grouper that he had named Goliath. I recognized the fish; it was taller than him and took up most of the picture frame. It was the big one that he fought to keep. Daddy loved deep-sea fishing. He had those long, fat fishing poles, a large tackle box, and a boat. He often said, "All a man needs to stay happy and live forever is a boat and the water."

Daddy was wrong again. He had all those things, and it did not cure his cancer. I didn't miss him, and I still hadn't cried.

SORRY FOR YOUR LOSS

I prayed for it, wished for it, and begged for it. So why did I feel so bad? Every night, I had prayed, hoping God would hear me, and He did. My prayers killed Daddy.

After the funeral, I stayed home from school for two weeks. Mama thought it was better for me to be home, giving me time to grieve. I was feeling fine, and I was bored. I spent some days at Mr. Tim and Ms. Millie's house. We pulled green tomatoes from their garden and fried them with peppers and onions. Ms. Millie worked around the kitchen, and I stood on a chair beside her at the stove. We talked about losing Daddy. She reassured me. "You are not alone. God has a bigger plan, and death is a part of that plan for everyone."

I wanted to tell her everything. *Yes, I know. I've been praying for this to happen. God and I are good friends, and He answered my prayers.* But I wasn't ready to discuss that yet.

Mornings were the only time I really noticed he was not around. The freedom of sleeping in on weekdays and waking up eager for school was something I didn't know I was missing. It was quieter in the house, and we no longer had to watch baseball on TV.

When I returned to school, I still had no tears for my loss. Some teachers wondered how I could be so joyful each day. Mrs. Simon pulled me aside during recess and asked if I needed time with the counselor to discuss my dad. Initially, I thought she must know my secret.

"No, I'm fine. I don't want to discuss it. He is dead, and I'm better now," I said. Those were the wrong words to use. Mrs. Simon looked shocked when I said, "I'm better now."

Later that day, they called me to see Mrs. Carson in the Guidance office.

"How are you feeling about losing your father?" she asked.

She felt I needed to discuss this.

"My dad wasn't a good man, you know? He had problems."

"Do you want to share what problems he had with me now?"

I told her everything. "He would threaten me never to tell anyone. So, I never did. You're the first human to hear this."

Mrs. Carson looked surprised. "What do you mean, the first human to hear this?"

"I have been telling God about my dad for years. I have been praying about it and wishing he would die. So, when I woke up that morning, and saw the paramedics working on Daddy's heart. I didn't feel scared. There was a calmness over me. I felt a sense of peace. My heart stopped shaking, and my mind stopped overthinking. I knew I would be okay from that night on," I admitted.

I attended counseling with Mrs. Carson each day during recess. She always asked a lot of questions, and I didn't mind answering them. I knew the truth would make her feel better.

"Why do you think being alone with Mr. Tim doesn't bother you?" she asked.

"I have thought about that. I wondered if all older men were like my dad. But I know I can trust Mr. Tim. He makes me feel safe," I said.

"What your dad did was not okay. He was wrong. This was not your fault," she said.

I knew that, but hearing someone else say it was good.

"Do I still need to see you now that you know everything?" I asked.

"No. Vivian. I can see that you are going to be fine. Stay as you are and always find someone you can trust to talk to. Talking to God is good, but you can also find a human."

That night, Mama came into my room. She seemed sad and said Mrs. Carson had called and told her about Daddy's secret.

"Don't be mad at Mrs. Carson. She's obligated to tell me about things like this. Why didn't you tell me when it was happening?" she asked.

I tried to explain, but I was afraid I'd hurt her feelings. "When Daddy threatened me, I knew you couldn't change it. You always listened to him and did whatever he told you. Liv was the only one who dared to talk back to Daddy. I thought about telling her. She and Billy got married and left, so I knew she couldn't help. Once I knew he had cancer, I realized God was taking care of Daddy for me."

Mama had no words; she just hugged me. We never discussed that side of Rodas again.

I stayed up late many nights thinking about him after he died. I wondered if Mama or Liv missed him. Was Mama lonely sleeping in her bedroom by herself? Who would walk me down the aisle or buy me my first car? Throughout the night of the funeral, I couldn't stop thinking about that sentence everyone kept saying to me. *I'm sorry for your loss.* I should have told them, "Don't be sorry for my loss— be sorry for his loss. He's the one who is missing out on my life."

Daddy, I am sorry for YOUR loss.

Part Three

Girl Power

My Baby

It was the end of sixth grade, and I turned 12 that summer. I never liked pies or cakes, but they were traditional for birthdays. My ideal birthday treat would have been macadamia nut and oatmeal cookies on the bottom layer and a five-story tower of iced donuts from Krispie K's bakery. Those were the best donuts ever! That would make for a happy birthday!

Mr. and Mrs. Cates had always been nice to me; they would wave to me when they saw me walking to and from the bus stop and sometimes gave me a ride home. If Mr. Cates stopped to offer me a ride in his truck, I would say yes and jump in the back. When he was driving the car, I had an excuse not to take the ride. I was uncomfortable alone in a car with any man.

"No thanks, it's a nice day out, and I enjoy walking," I lied.

Walking past his house, I would stop to pet his horses. Gypsy and Baby were Shetland ponies that belonged to his sons, although I'd never seen either ride them. Gypsy was white, and Baby was red with a black mane and tail. I liked Baby primarily because of her size. She was short like me.

"Do you want to learn to ride?" Mr. Cates asked. "Baby could use the exercise."

"I'll ask my mom and let you know." And still I wondered, *why ride a horse when I have a bike?*

After talking to Mama, she said learning to ride a horse would be fun.

Baby seemed to know when I would walk by each day, waiting at the fence line for me. Mr. Cates showed me where he kept the feed, leaving a carrot or apple as a treat for me to give her. I filled her and

Gypsy's water and food trays each night. On Saturday, I'd arrive early, and he would show me how to care for her.

In time, she came to trust me. When I put the bit in her mouth or tried to put on the reins, she stopped resisting. She was just the right height for me to jump on her back, and we spent our mornings together, riding in circles inside the pen. I serenaded her, and she would dance a graceful walk to the rhythm of my voice. Without my lead, she would go toward the barn when she felt tired and ready to stop. Softly talking to her, I gently stroked her nose, guiding my hand along her neck and back so she knew my touch and voice. She never kicked at me. Every day, with a hug and love, we became friends.

A few days later, I was riding her using a saddle. We had to stay within the fenced pen where she and Gypsy were kept. It was as though Gypsy could sense the comfort between me and Baby. Gypsy began running at me as I walked into the pen and nipping at Baby to get her attention. Her jealousy was evident. And still, Baby kept her walk steady.

That summer, I had my birthday party outside with streamers and balloons hanging from the red bee tree. All my friends from the neighborhood came over. Mama baked her favorite chocolate cake with chocolate icing. We played games: hide and seek and pin the tail on the donkey and I opened gifts. I could imagine nothing more to make me happier. At about that time, Mr. Cates walked from the backyard, leading Baby. Wearing a new saddle and bridle, she looked beautiful. Her long black tail was braided and adorned with green ribbons.

Mr. Cates handed her over to me. "She's all yours. You deserve her. I'll bring her food and fill the barrel each month for your mom. But you will need to feed her every morning and night and be sure she has water in the trough. Can you handle that?"

With tears, I said, "Yes, sir! I love her."

The Night Owl

Mama had a funny way of expressing herself. "Your sister is a baby bird that wants to fly and doesn't know how to use her wings."

"Let her go! Maybe the baby bird needs to fall out of the nest to learn," I said.

The Zipper was downtown's hottest nightclub. Liv loved going there on the weekends. Once Daddy was gone, she started hanging out with her friends again, returning to her old routine. She no longer needed to sneak out of the house. Mama laid down some rules, and they sat and talked it out whenever they had issues. Now that Daddy was gone, Mama didn't mind that I could listen in on their conversations, where before, she would ask me to go to my room while they talked. I took this as a sign that Mama realized my maturity.

"You're an example to your sister. She watches everything you do and will think it is okay to do those things," Mama said.

But I knew better. I had watched Liv play those games for years. She was an example for me to follow on what NOT to do. She worked at the local pizza place and would stay out late, smoke cigarettes in the house, and curse with every sentence. Sometimes, she and Mama argued, and Liv would storm out of the house.

"You dress like you have something to sell," Mama yelled as Liv slammed the door. I wasn't sure what that meant.

Liv slept late and came home late. We hardly ever saw her. And her weekend nights were all about the dance club. I admit she could dance and knew all the moves to the greatest songs. The music of Prince would play while she and Carol would dance to MTV's greatest hits, and I would join in. I realized I was missing out on some good fun and could not wait to go to The Zipper once I was older.

One night, after dancing at The Zipper, Liv came home with a great idea.

"I have figured out my career path, and I only need $250 to get started."

Mama and I exchanged raised eyebrows and shared curiosity about where this was headed.

"I want to start bartender school and get a job at The Zipper. They get great tips. I'm there every Friday and Saturday night; I may as well earn some money," she said.

Shaking my head, "Well, that is about the dumbest idea you've ever had."

A few weeks later, she was in bartender school. She was writing all the ingredients and drink names on index cards, and I was quizzing her to help her memorize them. She even let Mama and me taste a few of the drinks she made. We called it "research".

Liv was good at this. She took the test, passed, and got the job at The Zipper. I didn't think she could do it. I was proud of her, and Mama was too.

Liv was great at anything she set her mind to, but she would blow up when anything didn't go her way. This one time, Liv lost her temper and aimed most of her anger toward herself. She yanked her clothes from her closet, screaming, "I have nothing to wear on a date. Alan wants me to meet his parents before we go to the movies tonight."

"You have plenty to wear, you just don't like wearing clothes that cover your body," Mama said.

Shifting through Liv's closet, I could see. "She's right. She doesn't have the clothes for meeting his parents."

Still yelling at no one, she took the scissors, grabbed a chunk of her hair, and cut it above the shoulders. It looked awful. Seeing herself in the mirror only made things worse. When Mama saw what she had done, she quietly calmed her. Liv studied herself in the mirror and scrutinized the bad haircut she had given herself. She laughed, tears streaming down her face. I stood there staring at her in the mirror, hoping if I looked long enough, the hair would grow back. We all laughed. She looked horrendous!

"Let's go to the mall, find new clothes, and trim your hair. Next time, ask me to go shopping before you get upset. You could have handled this with all your hair still on your head," Mama said.

Working at The Zipper allowed Liv to meet many people. She would sometimes bring different girlfriends to the house to stay overnight. They would stay up late in her bedroom talking and smoking cigarettes.

I stood at her doorway one night and poked my head inside. "I can hear you talking, and you woke me up."

With a wave of her hand, she motioned me in. "Come in quick before Mama hears you."

They shared stories of their dance partners and tips earned from serving drinks.

"The more you flirt with the men, the higher the tip," Sharon said.

And Liv added, "They tip you better if you agree to whatever they say."

"Don't they know you don't care about them?" I asked.

"No, as long as their wives don't find out," Carol said.

And they all busted out laughing again.

Liv paid Mama back the money she borrowed for the bartender's classes and bought herself a car. She was doing it and she was becoming a career woman.

THE CHOICE

While Liv was living the nightlife, I was loving my days with Baby. I considered myself a professional cowgirl. We were used to each other's movements and personalities. She was a lot like me: quiet and meek. I would ride her down to the lake, jump off, and have her walk along the shoreline. She didn't enjoy getting her legs wet, but she allowed me to cool her off with splashes. We had built trust in each other, and I learned animals are more than pets; with love, they are family.

Shannon and I sometimes rode to the Sheriff's Posse to watch the local rodeo. She would borrow a horse from her Uncle Theo's stables, an Appaloosa named Fire. Shannon enjoyed riding him best because he was tall and had some attitude.

One early morning, as we were preparing to go to the Posse, her dad got up and helped us pack a bag with lunch, drinks, and snacks for us and the horses. We left just before dawn; the ride took two hours. Once there, we could let the horses rest while we enjoyed watching the rodeo. I wished I could ride a horse the same way those cowgirls did. The hairpin barrel was my favorite. Staying on the horse and guiding it around the barrels required speed and balance. I liked the clothing and braided pigtails that bounced as they galloped. By four o'clock, we knew we had to leave to get home. On this trip, we were riding down Tobacco Road; we stopped at a pond to let the horses have a drink.

They were building new houses, and certain areas had soft and wet ground. Shannon pointed and yelled, "Don't go there!" I misunderstood and thought she said, "Go over there."

Baby sank into the ground. The water started coming up on her legs, and she slowly descended. I panicked. My heart was racing, and I wasn't sure what to do, or how to help Baby or myself. I wanted to jump off her, but was afraid to leave her in the muck.

"Shannon! Help Me! We're sinking!" I cried.

Shannon jumped off her horse and went into rescue mode.

"Stay on the horse and throw me your reins, now!" she shouted.

I threw the reins at her, and she calmly pulled Baby towards her. With a long stick in her hand, she tapped Baby's legs for her to know which to pull out of the water. Shannon's tone changed, as she was careful not to yell at Baby or me. She continued to pull the reins, slowly guiding Baby to step out of each deep hole in the water and onto the solid ground.

I felt scared, and my heart was pounding. "Should I jump off now?"

"No! Stay on, you'll sink too if you jump down."

Once we were on the bank, Shannon helped me off Baby. She walked Baby around to ensure her legs were solid. As the sun set, we took a moment to relax. We knew we had to rush home before her dad would come looking for us.

It was always interesting how the horses sensed when we were close to home and quickened their pace to gallop toward home. I knew Baby was going to be okay.

There in the barn, we removed their saddles and changed their harnesses. Giving the horses a bath to cool them down from a day of exhaustion, Shannon and I agreed, we had another pact to keep. We told no one about that close call.

"You escaped quicksand," Shannon said.

"And you saved our lives."

I learned to listen and trust her judgment. But that was Shannon—she was always looking out for me. She was more than just a friend.

At the end of the summer, just before school started, Shannon came over. I knew something was wrong because I noticed her eyes were swollen and wet.

"My parents are getting divorced," she cried.

To my surprise. "How can they get divorced?"

I only knew one couple that had been divorced and that was

because Liv and Billy were too young. I assumed all parents with children were together forever.

"Not everyone stays married. Sometimes, divorce is better. Two happy homes are better than one that is not," Mama explained.

Shannon just cried. Feeling helpless as I watched her hurt. I was never comfortable hugging anyone to make them feel better, but with Shannon, I felt this urge to hold her. Mama and I reached out and comforted her while she wept.

After the divorce, William moved to North Carolina to live near the mountains, where he felt at home with nature. Wanda moved to Tampa. Shannon had to make the "divorce decision" that children face when parents separate.

"Choose which parent you would rather live with!? Kids shouldn't have to make that choice," I said.

I realized that this decision was going to affect me as well. I was losing my best friend.

Shannon returned a few days later.

"I've decided to live with my dad in North Carolina. I have never seen the mountains, and my parents agree it would be good for me to live with him. My mom said if I dislike it, I can always move back to her house."

Again, we both cried and talked about me coming to visit someday. I couldn't imagine any day without Shannon. At night, as I lay in bed, I cried. The pain was becoming real to me. It was the first time I grasped those words; *I am sorry for your loss.* I was losing Shannon forever.

When summer was over, she moved away. Their house had a sign in the yard that read, SOLD. Every time I rode Baby by their place, I would see that sign and gallop past their property. I could not believe how quickly they were gone. Memories of playing, camping, fishing, and cookouts were all I had.

William taught us to ride motorcycles by running beside us while we drove alone on the bike. "Brake, shift, slow down, go faster, shift, brake!" William shouted. Slowing down, he'd leap onto the seat behind us, bringing the motorcycle to a stop. We were too short to reach the ground, and I could barely touch the gears with my foot. This was one of my favorite things to do at Shannon's house.

Sometimes, he pulled a wagon on the back of the riding lawn mower. We'd lay in the wagon, dragging our hands to rake pine needles and toss them in. Whenever he hit a tree root, we flew out of the wagon, bouncing and laughing. He stopped for us to get back in. What would I give to do it again? She was my best friend. We shared so much more than fun times and memories. After she moved to North Carolina, I wrote her a letter.

Dear Shannon,
I can ride Baby much better now. I prefer riding her bareback. It's much easier and allows me to go faster. One day, we were riding past Mr. Cate's property, and Baby saw their horse, Gypsy. She neighed and waved her head. That got Baby so excited that she took off toward the fence. Baby stopped abruptly when she realized there was a ditch between us and the fence. She backed up a few steps and reared me off. I flew backward and hit the ground. Baby ran and jumped over the ditch. She wanted to be with Gypsy so badly that she reared me off. I couldn't get mad at her. Then, I realized that Baby and Gypsy were just like me and you. They, too, were best friends whose parents had split them up.
Write back soon. Best friends always, Vivi.

I continued writing letters to Shannon, but she said she was not much of a writer and eventually stopped. She sometimes called me on the weekends when her dad said the long-distance charges were cheaper. We only talked for five to ten minutes. Over time, we ran out of things to say.

QUANDO, QUANDO, QUANDO

Liv convinced Mama to attend The Zipper's dance banquet. I always knew Mama liked to dance. As she would play Latin music and move around the house with the mop or broom as her dance partner. She seemed happy in those moments and would play her favorite Engelbert Humperdinck eight-track and dance along. She had a beautiful singing voice, but I would never tell her that.

The morning after the dance, Liv and Mama sat at the kitchen table, laughing, drinking coffee, and smoking cigarettes. They were discussing their night at The Zipper. I sat there in shock as I listened to them describe a man Mama had met. They had this "singsong" name for him, "Rico es Rico," and laughed hysterically each time.

He invited Mama to dance, and he reserved each dance for her.

Mama shared their meeting. "We talked all night. It felt like I had known him for years. He was born in San Juan, Puerto Rico, and moved to New York with his parents when he was young," she continued, while she poured coffee and added sugar. "He retired from owning a construction company in New York this year."

She couldn't stop talking about him.

"He moved to Tampa to live closer to his children. He's been married twice and has a son and a daughter. Now he spends his time at the American Legion and does charity work for The Children's Hospital."

"He sounds great," I said with sarcasm. I felt jealous that Mama and Liv had something in common. And although I wanted Mama to be happy, I was hurt that I wasn't a part of it. She continued talking, while I nodded and tried to show my interest.

"He was there last Thursday, when he learned of the upcoming New Year's Eve party. Rico told Mama that Latin and disco were his favorite types of music," Liv said.

"Now those are my favorites, too." Mama laughed.

They both continued to entertain themselves. Their zealous cheerful tone annoyed me. I rolled my eyes and went to my room.

After Shannon moved away, I began spending more time with Carmen. She's two years younger than me and spends most of her time fishing. Her family lived at the end of Willowdale Road, where the cul-de-sac was. Her house was what they call an A-Frame design. The front faced the lake, with glass windows from top to bottom. During the weekends, her older brother Byron would take us on the boat, pulling us with the ski rope while we dangled off a tube. There we were, bouncing and gliding across the water. We enjoyed the heat of the summer without a care in the world.

One morning, she and her mom offered me a ride to the bus stop. "My parents will be at an American Legion event, so I'm inviting you and my cousin Madeline over."

I was so excited that I finally had a reason to use my new sleeping bag. As soon as Mama was home from work, I asked her, "Would it be okay for me to stay overnight at Carmen's house?"

Without hesitation, she approved. "Yes, of course. When you're at Carmen's house this weekend, let her father know you are friends with Rico."

George Ward owned Ward Construction. When he wasn't growing worms in the garden, he was the president of a construction company.

"George and Lisa Ward are members of the same committees and attend the same banquets Rico does. He knows George very well. And this year, you and Carmen can be in the Gasparilla Parade. Rico and George are on the same Krewe float in the Gasparilla."

That's a big deal, since you cannot be in the Gasparilla, unless you receive an invitation. I found myself liking Rico more.

In the evenings, I continued writing in my journal. Once I walked in on Mama putting my clothes away. She was struggling to close the drawer to my dresser. It was getting full, and clothes overflowed. I realized she would stumble upon my journals.

"Let me do that. I'll put my clothes away," I snapped, knowing I needed a new hiding space for my journals. I had noticed a framed cutout on the ceiling of my closet, but I would need a chair to reach it.

The next day, I asked Mr. Tim, "Do you have a hidden door in the ceiling of your closet?"

"Do you mean attic crawl space?" he asked.

"Is that what it's called? What is a crawl space for?"

"It's empty space in the attic, used for storage and access to the ductwork."

Usually, I would stay at Mr. Tim's while Mama was at work and Liv was out with friends. But I needed this time to hide my journals.

"I'll be back." I ran home and grabbed a stool and dragged it to my room. There, I pushed the hidden door up with my head. The heat and dust filled my face. It was dark.

This could work. I jumped down and grabbed my twelve completed journals. With a hug to my chest, *stay safe. I'll come back to you soon.* I placed them in their new home.

Part Four

Independence

New School, New Friends

Christmas vacation, or as the school called it, "winter break", was here. Except there was no winter in Florida. When I thought of winter, I imagined frigid days with snow, scarves, gloves, and coats.

It snowed once in Florida. I remember Mama waking me up that night to see the soft flakes falling. By the morning, a light blanket of white was on the ground. Schools closed; parents stayed home from work. I had the chance to wear my white furry coat and hat. The Tampa Tribune came out to take photos of Mr. Tim's yard. He had kept his sprinklers on all night so the water would freeze his garden and plants. When I went to his house in the morning, it was a "Frozen Cascade". That was what the newspaper called it. It was beautiful. His trees, bushes, grass, and garden were all frozen. The trees had icicles hanging down, and his yard was glowing white. I went to his yard, where some grass spots were slick enough for me to slide on like an ice skater. I had a wonderful day playing in the snow. Mr. Tim and I made small snowballs, and Ms. Millie made hot cocoa. The following day, it was all gone. Mr. Tim's yard had melted back to green, and he did not lose any plants or vegetables from the garden.

Winter break was usually two weeks, with no school. During that time, Mama took us to Montgomery Wards for Christmas shopping. I typically went through their catalog and picked out games and clothes I wanted. It was during our shopping trip that Mama shared the news.

"Shannon came home to her mother's house to celebrate Christmas, and she wants to see you," Mama said. "She has a surprise for you."

I was so excited, imagining what news she'd tell me: *She climbed a mountain, lives on a mountain, or was her school on the mountain?*

"Maybe she doesn't like living in North Carolina and is moving back to her mom's apartment," I guessed.

"No, that is not the surprise. Let's wait and see what she says."

I could see how she smirked and raised her brows; she knew.

Shannon and Wanda visited later that evening. We were excited, and it took us a few moments to stop jumping up and down at how much we'd missed each other. With all of our excitement, Shannon blurted out.

"Come live with me in North Carolina!"

Shocked, I leaned in, confused. "Wait, what? What did you say?"

With my ears, I'd heard her, but my mind insisted that couldn't be what she had said. I looked over at Mama and Liv, and they both were smiling. Everyone was looking at me, smiling and waiting for me to respond. I didn't know how to react. I finally gasped, "Oh, my God! Are you serious? You want me to move to North Carolina with you?"

It took me a few minutes to focus and understand Mama's words. "Vivian, do you want to move and live with Shannon and her dad in North Carolina?"

It felt like I was being forced to make "the choice". Pick between my mom or Shannon.

It was true. Being asked to move to North Carolina made me excited and flattered. However, I had no desire to go. Naturally, I agreed and showed excitement. I was a people pleaser and did not want anyone to be mad or disappointed.

I wished Mama had said *thank you for asking, but Vivian cannot move from home.* But that never happened. It seemed as though she wanted me to go.

I spent the week after Christmas saying my goodbyes to Mr. Tim, Ms. Millie, and Carmen. The hardest goodbye was to my horse, Baby.

∽

Mama asked, "Are you feeling nervous about the plane ride?"

"No. I'm just nervous about living somewhere new, not being here with you and Liv."

"This will be a great experience for you. When you want to come home, you can."

"Will I ever swim in the lake again? Who will feed Baby?" I wondered.

"Mr. Cates is coming to get her and take her back to his property while you are gone. You can move back when you want; she will still be your horse," Mama tried to sound convincing.

It was not until I said my goodbyes to Mr. Tim and Ms. Millie that I felt peace about moving. They always comforted me when I needed it.

"This is a good decision. You'll be okay, Little Bit. William's a good man, and he loves you. Ya hear?" Mr. Tim gave me a warm hug and held me. I felt his comfort and strength. It was calming.

"I baked you some cookies for your plane trip. You keep in touch, sweet Vivi," Ms. Millie hugged.

Liv seemed excited for me to go, too. "This will give Mama and me a place to go on vacation," she said, placing my clothes into the luggage.

Mama went on and on about how beautiful everything would be in North Carolina. "I always wanted to see the Smoky Mountains. Florida doesn't have waterfalls or mountainous views. Ay, Vivian, you are lucky for this experience," she continued.

Everyone was excited for me, so I chose to be excited, too.

I was thankful that I had enough space in the luggage to fit all of my books. Mama said she would have to cancel my book subscription, but I could sign up again once I was settled in North Carolina. She gave me a check for $200 to give to William.

"You'll need to buy winter clothes once you are there. The winters in North Carolina are colder than here, and you will need boots, a coat, gloves, hats, and scarves."

We went to Wanda's apartment in Tampa on New Year's Day.

"It's good that I live near the airport. I can drop you both off on my way to work in the morning. This will be fun for the two of you. You'll have each other now." Again, Wanda was another person offering encouragement where I was finding it hard to see.

I stayed up late the night before our flight, thinking about it. When I got nervous or scared, I would rub the scar on my hand and remember the secret Shannon and I had—our promise to be blood sisters forever. She was the one that I could go to whenever anything was challenging. On those mornings when I was scared to be alone, I knew I could count on her. Without her saying a word, I knew she needed me to be there for her now, in North Carolina. So, of course, I said, "Yes. I would love to move." Shannon and I flew together in an airplane for the first time.

Once we landed in Raleigh, North Carolina, William picked us up. He was pleased to see us both. The drive took over two hours to reach his house in Spring Mountain Valley. They lived in a small town where fields of nothing grew. A long driveway guided us to a big white house on the mountain. He had a large property with motorcycle trails winding up and down the hill, flowing creeks that fed into a small lake, and … a girlfriend named Darla.

She and William met at work, and she began staying overnight when Shannon went to Florida for Christmas. Shannon had difficulty getting used to seeing her father with a new lady friend. He seemed happier with Darla. Darla had a son named David. He was quiet and kept to himself, a year older than Shannon. They were both in high school, and I was starting junior high.

"The three of you will ride the bus together. Here, they have kindergarten through high school on the same property," William said.

We went shopping that weekend, and I picked out new clothes, a new coat, and, my favorite, a new pair of black boots built for snow and rain.

The fashion there was different. Everyone wore a tee shirt under a plaid shirt, which they called "a flannel". When it got too warm, I took the flannel off and tied it around my waist. Blue jeans tucked into boots was the look everyone wore. Girls with long hair usually tied it up in a bun or ponytail.

"I've never put my hair up before," I said.

Darla brushed my long thin hair and explained, "Hair ties are an accessory and must match your outfit."

I was impressed with how many colors a hair tie could come in.

She twisted and yanked with a flick of her wrist as she pulled my hair up into a bun. I glared at myself in the mirror, and for the first time, I noticed the shape of my face and neck. How much I looked like a ballerina with a tight bun on top.

Some mornings, she would braid my hair in pigtails, just like the cowgirls wore. For the first time, I smiled at myself. *I looked pretty.*

It was the first day of school. Shannon was feeling ill and could not go. David and I rode the bus together, but then he parted with his friends.

He pointed to the gym. "Go inside and find the sign assigned to your class."

Upon entering, I was met with a chaotic scene of people shouting and running in all directions. I spotted the signs and discovered the one that said: Seventh grade, Team of the Knights.

"Hi, I'm Vivi. Is this where I need to sit for Mr. Knight's class? Today is my first day."

The tall cheerleader holding the sign introduced herself as Trisha, "Hello, Vivi. I love your name. Yes, all seventh graders on Mr. Knight's team sit here. We'll go to the team after the rally finishes."

There were cheerleaders shouting as they energized the crowd with music and dance. The basketball and wrestling team members came running in. The staff members greeted everyone returning from the winter break and cheered on the new semester! After the rally, we followed Trisha with her sign in hand.

"Mr. Knight, this is your new student, Vivi."

North Carolina differed from Florida in many ways. The air smelled sweeter; the trees looked like skinny-dead gray arms reaching toward the sky. Even the water flowing from the mountain seemed louder. When driving, the streets were like roller coasters over the rise and fall of the hills. There was nothing but grass and fields for miles. Liv was right; it was beautiful.

People at school were friendly and for my first week, I seemed to fit right in. Everything was similar to home, except for one thing I noticed. They had an accent and sounded like Mr. Tim. A twang was in their voice, and I would have one too, by the month's end.

The Hills Are Alive

Four teams made up the seventh grade. They didn't call them classes here. The teams were in one giant room, and an accordion-style wall separated each section. We kept the walls open when the four teams worked together and closed them during tests or quiet times. I was on Team Three with Mr. Knight. He was short, thin, blond, with blue eyes, and a little quirky. He wore a collared shirt with a tie and dress pants. So far, he was my favorite teacher I had ever had. When we had quiet time, he liked to refer to paintings of famous artists and play classical music — he was brilliant. He did not have an accent; he was from Michigan.

Quiet time was my favorite time. We read or caught up on homework. We went to the library once a week and chose as many books as we wanted from any genre. My favorites were mystery and drama, and I was working on *Bridge to Terabithia* and *Tuck Everlasting*.

Since there was an extensive library at school, I decided I no longer needed to subscribe to books in a box anymore. Mr. Knight was always recommending a new book and seemed to know my style of reading.

For the first time, I experienced the change of classes per period. It was during those transitions in the hallway that I noticed the posters on the walls.

One poster stood out from the others. A man with white hair wearing a top hat in colors of red, white, and blue. His finger pointed out to me: 'Uncle Sam Wants You to be a hall monitor.'

"Would you refer me to the office to sign up?" I asked Mr.

Knight.

"No, I don't think so. I have another idea to offer you. We are still discussing the details, but I'll tell you more about it soon," he said.

I missed Mama and Liv on the weekends. Usually on Saturday, whenever I called the house, Liv answered. "I knew you would call today," she said. "Mama's not here. She spends the weekends at Rico's house and comes home on Sunday nights. You should call on Sundays instead."

Liv told me how nothing had changed. "Mr. Cates is taking good care of Baby. Mr. Tim waves and asks, 'how's my Little Bit doin' in the Carolinas.' Mr. Powell came over and offered us some RC Cola. He said he had too many now that you weren't here to drink it." We laughed.

When I got off the phone with Liv, I called Mr. Tim. Ms. Millie answered and stopped me halfway to hand the phone over.

"Hold on, sweetie, Mr. Tim has been dying to talk to you," she said.

"Hey, there, Little Bit. How ya doin'?" he said.

And just like that, his voice brought me home. I told him everything, from the first day of school to the sounds of the waterfalls, jumping rocks in the river, and how I wished I had brought my fishing pole and horse.

"It's a good thing I don't have a bicycle here because there are too many mountains; I don't think I could ride up these hills. But if I had Baby here, she and I could run everywhere."

Mr. Tim gave out a laugh and warmed my heart. He was genuinely happy to hear my voice, and he showed an interest in my stories.

"Next Saturday, I'll call you instead so that the long-distance charge won't cost anything to William."

"Oh yes. That would be great. If I can talk to you on Saturdays, I can call Mama on Sundays."

I asked him for his address and if it would be okay for me to write letters to him and Ms. Millie. Mama and Liv took a long time to reply to my letters. I had been writing to Carmen, too. She was the only one who wanted to write back. She shared her and her dad's fishing adventures, and the stories of seeing the "four-footer", who she thought was now a "five-footer".

My team was writing letters and reaching out to another seventh-grade team in Michigan. Mr. Knight called it the Pen Pal Project. This project aimed to improve our writing skills, and Mr. Knight would accept the letters we wrote as a quiz grade.

I wonder, if I let him read my letters to Mr. Tim, if he would claim that as extra credit?

On Sunday, I called Mama. She answered the phone on the first ring. She seemed excited to hear my voice.

"Ay, Vivian, you sound so much older."

"I stay busy with schoolwork. I like my classes and teachers. We attend church every week, and I am a part of the youth group. They have plans to take a trip over Spring Break. Although I miss you very much, I am having a wonderful time here," I said.

"Ay, mi amor. I miss you so much, too. But I am so happy to hear you are enjoying yourself. Continue to have fun. You deserve this time. God bless you, mi amor. Call me again next weekend and tell me about your week. I enjoy hearing your stories."

We hung up. Despite missing her, I realized that moving here had been a good idea.

Everyone attended church on Sundays and met for lunch at the local diner after the service. I saw a lot of my friends there. We sat around talking about school and boys. The girls liked to gossip about other girls, and the boys liked to talk about sports.

My new best friend was Debbie. She was on my team and we sat together everywhere we went. Her family also went to the same church as us. She and I had a crush on the Crawford twins. They were in Team Two.

During the week, I stayed busy with school and chores at home. My chores around the house were keeping my room clean and vacuuming. On the weekends, we helped William outside. On Sunday, we went to church. Staying busy kept my mind off of home. I missed Mama, mostly at bedtime. When Shannon, David, and I went upstairs to bed, they usually kissed and hugged their parents' good night. At those times, I missed Mama most and wished I were home.

"Good night, Vivi. Don't stay up too late reading," William

shouted as I walked upstairs.

Springtime in the Carolinas was a beautiful time of year. The weather was still cold, but the snow was melting, allowing fresh growth to peek through the trees.

Back at home, all the trees were green. Here, the trees bloomed with blossoms of different shades of pink, lavender, and yellow, as though pastel candies were thrown into the sky. A cool breeze would blow and the loose blossoms would fill the sky. Everything here was more colorful.

Our church youth group was going on a ski trip for spring break. We had the week off school, and Mama was still sending money to William to help with my part of living here.

Fellowship sent a permission slip for me to go on the Boogaloo Ski trip. William called Mama and asked her if she was okay with me going.

"It's a good deal, Mom, for only $200 including my meals, two nights in the resort, ski clothes, boots, and ski rental. My best friend, Debbie, is going too. Her dad is going as a chaperone."

"You sound excited! Of course, you can go. Is Shannon going too?" Mama asked.

"No. this trip is for the Junior High youth group only."

The church youth groups were split in two. With so many students in the seventh and eighth-grade level, the trips were divided between spring and winter. That night, I started packing my bag. I noticed Shannon wasn't happy, and I could sense her jealousy.

"Are we still best friends?" she asked.

"Of course we are. You'll always be my best friend. To me, you're like a sister."

"Since you moved here, you seem different, and I overheard you telling your mom that Debbie is your new best friend. Is that true?"

"Yes, Debbie is my best friend at school. She helps me not to miss my friends back in Florida."

Shannon gave a nod, she understood and remembered her friends back in Florida, too. With scarred hands, we exchanged high fives, and I reassured her, "Our bond is unbreakable."

It took us over three hours to arrive at Boogaloo Ski Resort. The bus ride was fun.

We sang songs and played trivia along the way. Debbie and I sat next to the Crawford twins. She liked Kable, and I noticed Kischen was paying me attention. He gave me compliments. I understood that this was what they referred to as *flirting*. It was new to me. I had never noticed boys this way. They were always brats that got in the way of me having fun with my friends. I had always looked at boys as rough and loud. They liked to run and compete with everyone they played with. And they smelled like stale trash. Their hair was always messy, and they didn't care if they burped or passed gas loudly. I was always confused about why Liv liked boys with all those gross habits. That day, I understood.

When we arrived, we met Kelly. She was our weekend guide and chaperone while we were in the cabins. She led us on a campus tour and informed us about the extremely cold weather.

"Always wear your winter cap and jacket when you step outside and travel with a buddy," she said.

Because we were in the mountains, there was wildlife everywhere. There were signs that reminded us, "Do Not Feed the Wildlife," with a picture of a bear and a coyote.

I raised my hand. "Are there actual bears and coyotes here?"

"Oh yes! You will find many wild animals here in the forest. A reminder, we are in their home, so give them respect," Kelly said.

At the main lodge, we collected our ski gear. I chose a neon-green jacket, black overall pants, goggles, gloves, and ski boots. They handed me my skis, and we went to the beginners' class. Everyone had to take the training class if they were under sixteen. I found that skiing on a flat surface was more enjoyable than the fear of riding the lift and descending the mountain.

Kischen and Kable had done this before, so they were already at the top of the mountain. We gave them time to get ahead before we went toward the lift. This was all so new to me; rising above the mountain, sitting on the bench as the conveyor pulled us toward the snowy tops. I imagined the snow caps as those large-brimmed hats

Mr. Tim wore when working in the yard.

As we shimmied upward, I saw the trees that seemed so small below me. It was stunning. Mama would have loved this. I giggled at the thought of her words, *"Ay, mira que linda."*

Once we were at the top, we realized the mountain was below us. My hands were shaking as we hopped off the bench and began gliding. My heart was pounding as I maneuvered my legs and feet together. It was easier than I thought, but I was glad to have my poles for balance. I planted my feet on the ground and held my balance. The icy wind froze my face as I slid down the hill, and the only way down was on my skis. I constantly reminded myself to open and close my feet to adjust my speed and to keep shifting my legs from side to side.

I was skiing in the snow! Reaching the bottom of the hill, I raised my hands out of pure excitement, and losing balance, I fell. And still, Debbie and I cheered; we were both so happy! The hours flew by as we continued on the green trails until we decided it was time for some hot cocoa to warm ourselves. Inside the restaurant, we found Kischen and Kable and shared a table for lunch. Afterward, the four of us took a few trips down the mountain together. Debbie and Kable went ahead, and although I thought Kischen was cute and kind, it was evident that we were only there to be supportive friends to them.

When the weekend was over, we were back on the bus and headed home. I stared out the window and waved to the trees. The mountains in the Carolinas had moments of flowing waterfalls that reminded me of Mr. Powell's long white beard. Kischen and Kable were asleep in the seat next to us, and Debbie was asleep on my shoulder. I couldn't sleep because my mind was racing about all that I had accomplished since leaving Florida. This was an experience I never thought I would have. I was glad I made the right choice.

Monday, when we returned to school, there was a shift in me. I felt a part of the school community, and I had more confidence. I was no longer a stranger to those in the hallway.

Mr. Knight requested two volunteers to be his student aides.

"We are offering a new program called VA–Volunteer Aides.

These students will work together to assist me with my weekly schedules, lesson plans, and grading papers. I am looking for two students, one from the seventh grade and one from the eighth grade. Please see me after class if you are interested," he announced.

Immediately after class, I approached his desk.

"I am very interested in the VA position."

"Good to know. I'll add your name to the list. I plan to make final decisions by the end of the day."

I kept it a secret that I had entered my name; I knew to become a VA student, you must replace one of your MAP classes, music, art, or physical education with it.

After lunch, I would usually go straight to music class. Mrs. Wright called out to me as I entered the room. "Congratulations, Vivi! You can go to Mr. Knight's class now."

Walking toward his room, I saw Danny Bullet in the hallway.

Danny was the most popular boy in the junior high building. He was gorgeous, with deep brown hair and blue eyes. I noticed his broad shoulders and stocky build. I could tell that he worked out. He dressed differently than the other boys. He wasn't one to wear the plaid flannel shirts; instead, on a chilly day, he had a nice sweater with a collared shirt peeking out the neckline. His wavy brown hair, with a side part, gave him that preppy look. I finally knew what Liv meant when she said, 'one day you'll find a guy who fits your taste.' I didn't realize I had a taste … until *now.*

As I entered, Mr. Knight was already talking to Danny.

"Hello, Vivi. Come on in. With both of you here, I want to congratulate you both on becoming my VA students for the rest of this year. After lunch each day, you will come to my class, and we will work together on various duties I need help with. We are starting this new program, and if it goes well, we will continue it for future school years."

Danny was in the eighth grade. I had seen him walking in the hallways in between classes. He was always with the popular girls, the cheerleaders. He was on the wrestling team. So, of course, I was surprised to see that he also wanted to be a VA.

We would arrange the seating in the class, open or close the partitions, grade papers, make Xerox copies, and help Mr. Knight as needed. Being in Danny's presence was all I cared about, regardless of the activity. Here we were, talking to each other while no one was in the room. Mr. Knight would use this time to eat his lunch. I told Danny I was from Florida and left my family and horse to move here to live with my friend. And, of course, I was mature enough to be on my own. He shared that he was originally from Indiana, but had moved here when he was ten.

"What do you do when you're not at school?" he asked.

"I enjoy fishing, riding go-carts, motorcycles, and hiking," I said.

He stopped moving the desks around and looked at me.

"You like fishing and motorcycles?"

"Well, yes, I ride all the time. We live on a mountain near a creek, and I fish down at Cooper's Lake."

I wasn't sure why he thought that would be surprising.

"Wow. You don't look the type. I figured a Florida girl was a city girl," he said.

I smiled and kept working. As the weeks passed, we got to know each other better and realized that we had things in common. Danny told me about his home back in Indiana. His family had a farm. They raised field corn for animals.

"Did you know there are different types of corn for people and animals?" he asked.

"No, I didn't know there was a difference."

I lied. Of course, I knew corn for feed was not for humans. But he was so interested in telling his story that I didn't want to sound like a show-off.

Each day, we did our work while we sat and talked. We became friends. I looked at Danny differently now that I knew him. We smiled at each other and joked in conversation. He tapped me on the arm and gave a soft touch when he gestured to me.

Each time he touched my arm, I felt a shiver down my neck. A few times, I touched him and wondered if he felt the shiver too.

I admit I had a crush and wondered if Danny felt anything. It was a Friday when he took me by surprise.

"Vivi, would you wanna hang out at next Thursday night's football game?"

I didn't know how to react. I looked behind me, thinking that he was talking to someone else, and realized that we were the only two in the room. And there it began: I was friends with a popular boy.

I couldn't wait to get home and ask. "Darla, would it be okay for me to go to the junior varsity football game, and can I buy a school shirt? Everyone wears them to school on Thursdays. I can stay in Mr. Knight's room after school and attend the game."

"Sure, I can pick you up after."

AGAINST THE WIND

That weekend, I called home. I was excited to tell Mama and Liv about everything going on with me at school. Liv answered, and they both listened as I told them about my ski trip and I shared how we stayed in cabins in the mountains. They were happy for me and told me more about Rico and the various locations they would go to dance. He was taking her to Puerto Rico for her birthday next week. Liv told me about this new guy that she met at The Zipper.

"His name is Carter, and he is five years older than me. He has an actual job as a salesman. I have been staying with Carter while Mama is at Rico's."

"That sounds great. I'm glad you are both doing well."

I sounded supportive, but inside, I kept waiting for it to fall apart. Because it always did.

Shannon and I were becoming more distant. I continued to save a seat for her when I got on the bus, but each time she walked past. I peeked back to watch her sit beside a boy who would make her laugh. That was when I realized that while I missed my friend; she was moving on. Our friendship had changed.

It was a few days later when she stopped at my seat as I scooched over for her to sit; she leaned down and said, "Don't mention Jacob to my dad or Darla. Best friends keep secrets."

"Of course, I would never …," my words trailed, she continued towards the back of the bus.

When we were home, we didn't talk. Both Darla and William

could sense the distance between us.

"Is everything okay? Is there anything you want to talk about?" Darla asked.

I was unsure what she wanted to hear. "No, I'm fine."

I was so excited all week. Each day, I worked on my homework to stay caught up. I wanted nothing to get in the way of Thursday night football. We met at Mr. Knight's classroom.

"The concessions are open before the game begins, so do you want to walk and grab something to eat?" Danny asked.

We were having a nice dinner and conversation, about to get up and walk toward the bleachers.

"Oh good, Lauren and Robbie are here. I can introduce you," he said. "Vivi, this is my girlfriend Lauren and her brother Robbie."

It was then that I realized he saw me as just a friend. I didn't know that he had a girlfriend. You would think "a girlfriend" would have come up in our many talks. When he touched my arm and laughed at my jokes, he could have mentioned "a girlfriend".

Lauren was pretty. She had long blonde hair and green eyes. She was wearing a top that was too small for her chest and a skirt that was too short for her long, skinny legs. I glanced at her brother, Robbie, who was one year younger than me. I noticed he was dressed fancier than me. Seeing the three together made me stop and look down at my school tee shirt and faded jeans with black boots. I had never looked at myself as less than, or felt it, until now.

"You're right. She is simple and plain." Lauren giggled.

I tugged at my tee shirt and with sarcasm, "Oh, this? Well, I dressed for the game and dirty bleachers. I didn't know we were going to go dance in a nightclub."

Who was I kidding? I felt humiliated as we stood there waiting in line to climb the stairs to our school section on the bleachers. Lauren continued talking, but I wasn't listening.

"It would be nice having someone to hang out with next year when we transfer here. By then, you won't need Danny to tutor you in math," she said.

I stopped, turned around, and stared directly at Danny. He

looked confused and embarrassed. He said nothing. I realized what was happening.

"Is that what he told you? He was tutoring me. You're right, I won't NEED Danny by then." I was angry. I made my way back to the school and called Darla. "Can you come pick me up now? My friends bailed on the game, and I don't want to be alone," I lied.

During the drive home, while I listened to the radio, one of my favorite Bob Seger songs, *Against the Wind,* played. The words and music brought my thoughts back to how much I missed home.

I sat alone in my bedroom and contemplated why I was here. My family lived in Florida with all my friends back at school, and the people who cared about me back home on Willowdale Road. I called Liv and Mama, but no one answered. I remembered Rico was taking her to Puerto Rico this week. Summer was right around the corner. It was time for me to go back home. I would love to be back by June to celebrate my birthday.

Danny and I continued to work together in Mr. Knight's class. However, now we'd only discuss the projects we were working on. I misinterpreted his flirting and kindness and felt angry at myself for assuming he liked me. I would use the weekend to relax and call Mama and ask her about moving home.

I spent the entire weekend reaching out to Mama and Liv, but they didn't respond. Finally, on Sunday night, Mama answered. I could tell something was wrong. She did not sound like herself.

"What do you mean, you're selling our house?!" I shouted. "What's going on? Is everything okay with Liv and you? Is someone sick?"

"No, no, everyone here is fine. I have some news for you. I've told you I sometimes stay with Rico at his home in Tampa, so we can go dancing. We have decided to live together, and I am planning to move to his house full time," she said.

"Does that mean Liv will be in our house alone? How can she afford that?"

"No. No. Olivia is living with her boyfriend, Carter. They are serious and talking about getting married next year. You will like him; he treats Olivia very well."

I was furious and could not help but shout.

"Mama, what are you doing? I want to come home. I don't like it here anymore. Shannon and I are not friends like we used to be, and I don't fit in at this school. Aren't I still your daughter? Can I come home?" I begged.

She stayed calm.

"Yes, of course," Mama assured me. "I'll see what I can do to make plans for you to come home."

"Okay, thank you." We said goodbye and hung up. I continued to sit there, both hurt and angry. The tears would not stop.

With only one month of school left, summer was right around the corner. During the period that Danny and I were in Mr. Knight's class, I would work on homework and catch up on my reading. Mr. Knight noticed that we were no longer talking to each other.

"Is everything okay with you and Danny?"

"We are friends, but I don't think his girlfriend likes me. So, I am keeping my distance."

"Oh, he has a girlfriend?"

"Yup! I said the same thing," with a smirk and a smile.

The last day of school finally arrived, and I was eager for its end. I even told Mr. Knight I was happy to have had him as my teacher, but I would be returning to Florida this summer.

He looked disappointed.

"Well, Vivian, I will tell you I have enjoyed having you in my class and getting to know you as my assistant. If I had a daughter, I'd want her to be like you."

He handed me a gift that he had wrapped. It was a silver engraved bookmark with a green ribbon tied on the top. It read:

To one of my favorite students,
You are kind, friendly, and true -
In all my years of teaching,
I am glad to have met you.
—— Your friend and teacher, Mr. Knight

I left his class with a smile and a sense of accomplishment. I felt a sense of pride in myself.

After the last bell rang, the hallways filled with students rushing. I visited my locker one last time to retrieve my flannel and book bag. I had already turned in all my textbooks. There in my locker was a piece of paper folded up. I opened it and could see that it was a letter from Danny.

Vivi,

If I hurt your feelings, I apologize. I never intended to do that, and I didn't want the summer to come without telling you. Over the past month, I've missed joking with you and hanging out in class. I hope you and I can talk and see a movie together over the summer.

Danny

I folded the note and placed it in my pocket. As I walked toward the buses, I caught myself smiling. The time had come, and I was glad to say goodbye to this school. I followed the line of buses and searched for mine. There, waiting for me outside the bus door, was Danny.

"Did you get my letter?"

"Yes, I got it, thanks."

"Can we talk?" he asked, motioning to the back as we walked.

The last day of school brought more rowdiness than usual. Kids ran in different directions, yelling out bus windows at each other. We went behind the bus, where it was quieter.

"Like I said in my letter, I am sorry if I hurt you. I couldn't tell if you liked me or were just being friendly."

Standing with him face to face made me nervous. We had spent every day alone in a room, but now we stared silently at each other, out in the open. He looked at me with big blue eyes peeking out from his tousled dark hair.

"It's usually easy for me to tell when a girl likes me because they make it obvious, but I couldn't tell that with you." His face gave a curious look, as if he were waiting for me to speak. I stood there quietly, afraid to move, unsure of what to say now.

"I um, do. I do like you. After spending so much time with you in class, it was nice having our talks. We had so much in common, but then you surprised me with a girlfriend. And I knew I couldn't tell you how I felt," I said.

"Can I kiss you?"

I couldn't speak, so I nodded. Danny kissed me. Twice.

He wrapped his arms around me and hugged me tightly. When he finally let go of me, I looked into his beautiful eyes.

"Oh, wow! I must tell you something. I'm moving back to Florida this summer."

He looked surprised and sad, and I wanted to take it back.

I could call my mom and tell her I changed my mind.

"I'll miss you," he said, and he hugged me again.

We heard the bus start the engine, and I hurried towards the door. His bus was parked next to mine, and I saw him move to his seat. He waved his hand, and I waved back. I remembered his letter was in my pocket, and I read it again and again. I leaned my head on the window, and tears filled my eyes. And with a smile I whispered, *that was my first kiss.*

HOMECOMING

My birthday was three days away.

"I will get you home before the July Fourth company picnic," Mama promised.

My books were the one thing I knew I had to pack. I was not expecting anything for my birthday since I had limited space. I missed Shannon already. She and I only shared small talk at this point. Her boyfriend visited often, and they would go hiking and fishing in the lake. I avoided asking to go with them so I wouldn't become a burden. I enjoyed relaxing under the tree and resting in the hammock. It faced the mountain behind the house, and you could hear the creek flowing on a quiet day. By far, this was my favorite place to read. I had taken a nap or two in that hammock. I should have asked for one for my birthday. Of course, there were no mountains in Florida for the perfect view.

The mornings there were calm and peaceful. I liked that about William's house. It was easy to see that Shannon was much like her father. They were both soft-spoken and gentle-hearted. That was why she and I got along so well. I learned a great deal from being with her and William.

"Vivi, once you and Shannon are ready, we'll go into town for a few things, and we can have lunch at Mr. Al's," he said.

Mr. Al's was one of the best barbecue places in town. The meat was tender, and the barbecue sauce was homemade. William bought several bottles with a range of sweet, tangy, and spicy flavors. He knew I enjoyed having it at home for chicken grill night.

While shopping, I collected some puzzle books and my favorite

Search-a-Word and crypto quotes. I enjoyed a fresh pen for starting a new puzzle book. I chose some stationery with a monogrammed letter "P" to match my last name on the top of each page. Once I moved back to Florida, I planned to write to Shannon again. If she missed me, she would write back.

We got home after four o'clock, and as we walked through the kitchen door, I saw Mama standing there. Liv came walking from around the corner.

"Surprise! Happy Birthday!" they screamed.

It all took me by surprise, indeed! My birthday was in two days. I was happy to see them both, and I didn't realize how much I had missed them. Tears fell as Mama hugged me and said, "Feliz Cumpleanos, mi amor."

"We drove here for your birthday and will drive home together the day after," Liv said.

"Oh, wow! We're going home in three days?" I was careful not to sound too excited to be leaving. When I looked at Shannon, she lifted her gaze to meet mine. She was sitting alone on the sofa, keeping a distance. Her eyes were low, and I felt that way too.

I snuggled up to her and said, "I'll miss you the most. Guess who kissed me?"

She looked at me, and with a grin, she mouthed, "Danny?"

I could only smile and nod. We both burst out in laughter. There, everything was better.

"You better write to me," I said.

She nodded. "I will, I'll miss you too."

We all gathered in the living room and discussed my past six months in North Carolina. William and Darla bragged about how I made new friends, joined the youth group at church, and learned to snow ski.

"I want to thank William and Darla for allowing me to live here. My time here was a great experience where I discovered a lot about myself. I made some great memories that I will carry forever." I thanked my mom for allowing me to move away.

Shannon and I had another secret we both held on to. I told no one else about Danny and my first kiss.

On June 11, we celebrated my 13th birthday with chocolate cake and vanilla icing. William and Darla gave me green luggage, and I filled it with all my new clothes and books. It was a nice, quiet day with just us celebrating. These were my actual favorite people, and I called them family.

We got up early the following day and packed the car.

"We want to keep going until we reach home," Liv said.

I sat in the backseat and worked on my puzzles. I wrote Shannon a letter and even started another journal where I wrote about my first kiss with Danny. When we finally got through Georgia, I was excited to see the sign: *Welcome to Florida, The Sunshine State.*

Coming Home

I was home in Florida, but not to the home I remembered. Mama waited until we were driving on the road to tell me. She'd sold our house on Willowdale Road and moved to Tampa with Rico. I felt devastated.

When I asked about my horse, Baby, she said that Mr. Cates was able to find a young family to take her.

"I knew you were thinking of selling our house, but I didn't realize you had already sold it," I cried.

"Yeah, someone offered us a good deal. I couldn't let it pass. Besides, Rico has a big enough home for us. You will like it there."

Once we arrived at Rico's house, I had my own bedroom with boxes piled inside. Mama packed my room, and I was grateful she threw nothing away. I rushed to open the boxes and shuffled through them. I was looking for the one thing I knew would still be in our house on Willowdale Road. My heart sank when I realized they were not inside these boxes. I had hidden them so well that only the new owners would find them.

Then Mama asked, "Are you looking for these?" She was holding a box wrapped in Christmas paper.

I continued pulling items out of the boxes, scurrying through things I hadn't seen in months. Ignoring the box in her hand, I shrugged and said, "No, I just had something I was hoping made the move."

"I wrapped them in Christmas paper so Liv and Rico would think they were Christmas decorations. Nobody has seen them." Mama lifted the lid to the box, and there inside were my twelve journals.

"How did you know?"

"Ay, Vivian. I used to be a young girl, too, and I loved to write. Mr. Tim came to the house when he saw we were moving. He told me you asked about a 'crawl space' in the closet. When I checked inside your closet, there they were," she said.

I cried—not just because I didn't lose them, but because Mr. Tim knew to save them.

Living with Rico in Tampa gave me the advantage of the local library being within walking distance. I found a pamphlet from the American Red Cross seeking volunteers.

"Can I? The age is for anyone thirteen and older," I said.

"Sure, if you think you would like that," Mama said.

I signed up and turned in the pamphlet. A few days later, Mama received the phone call, and we went down to a local nursing home where they assigned me a uniform and workstation.

Mama and Rico would drop me off in the mornings and pick me up in the afternoons. My schedule was for the rest of the summer, Monday through Wednesday, from 9am to 2pm. I enjoyed the time, answering telephones, passing out food trays, reading to the residents, and assisting with Bingo in the community room.

Once school started, I began volunteering on Saturdays. Sometimes a resident would pass away. It was heartbreaking to see their families losing a loved one. And some residents didn't have anyone to claim their bodies. We would have a small service for them in the chapel. While working there, I fully understood what "I am sorry for your loss" truly meant.

In August, Liv, then twenty-one, married Carter James Lawson. They bought a house near Rico's place. I thought it was great to run over when I needed time away from Mama and Rico. There were many rules while living at his house. He was what Mama called "disciplined" and what I called "strict".

Liv and Carter were cooking fried potatoes one day while I was visiting.

"I love these papita fritas," I said as I picked a few from the bowl. "You thought living with Daddy was tough when you were my age; you should try living with Rico."

I tried to explain to Liv, but she defended Rico.

"See things from his point of view, too, Vivi. He is taking in a teenager at his age," she argued.

Liv tried to convince me that this was difficult for Rico, but I didn't have it. "Why would a 66-year-old man be involved with a woman who has a teenager? And why does Mama only date old men?"

Carter smirked and lifted his eyebrows. "She has a point."

"Can you please stop eating the papitas until I have them all cooked? And Vivi, you should be patient with him. He loves you and Mama," Liv said. "And, if you want the truth, comparing Daddy to Rico is like comparing King Kong to the King of England!"

And Carter was right there for the win. "There is no King of England; do you mean the Queen?"

Carter and I laughed, and Liv gave us both the look of death.

"Why don't you talk with your mom and Rico and let them know how you feel? Write out your issues and let them see what you need?" Carter suggested.

We stared at Carter, dumbfounded, as if he had sprouted a second head.

"What? Why would you say that? No one talks to their parents about their issues," Liv said.

I nodded and agreed. "Yeah, Carter, we've never talked to our parents about our problems. I wouldn't know how to do that."

Pointing to the desk, Carter said, "Hand me a piece of paper."

Intrigue filled me as Carter took the paper and, with a pencil, drew a line down the center of the page. At the top of the left side, he wrote I WANT, and on the top of the right side of the page, he wrote YOU WANT.

"Now, starting on this side, list each thing you want while living with them. For instance, you want a curfew for what, 10 pm?"

"No, I want to go to bed at 11 o'clock, but they want me in bed by 10 o'clock," I said.

"Then, put that down," he pointed.

I began my list. It included my curfew to be in the house and curfew to bed.

"I'm okay doing my chores, but I want Sundays with no chores. When I lived up north with William, we didn't have chores on Sundays. William said Sunday is God's Day. Rico said the house is a mess every day, not just on the days I want."

"Write that down; I want and you want."

I continued to write. This made me feel like I was making progress, which was thrilling.

"At the end of your list, put your willing-to-agree ideas. That means you will take the 11 pm bedtime and agree to get up for school with no issues."

"Ooh, that is good. I'm going to write that down," I continued.

"Am I going to show them this list or say all this to them?"

He explained, "If you want to be involved in the decision-making process and express your needs, you'll have to present this to them and speak up for yourself."

"He is brilliant! Man, I wish you had married Liv when Daddy was around. We could have used you back then."

I started for the door. Liv called out, "Wait, finish the list here. I want to read it when you're done."

With so much excitement, I wanted to hurry and get this done.

"Sorry, Liv, this one is mine. You'll have to make your own list. Thanks, Carter, you're the best," I said as I ran out the door. I didn't wait to eat dinner.

Part Five

Teen Years

SUNSHINE FOR MILES

The beaches! You could not live in Florida without having gone to the beaches. I've visited Miami Beach and experienced its vibrant rhythm and lights that the city offered. Daytona was where you could drive your vehicle along the shore and up toward Jacksonville Beach was where you could find some quiet time. Northerners liked the west toward the Panhandle town of Fort Walton Beach, where one could see and feel the soft powdery sands. But by far, the best beaches were from Clearwater to Saint Petersburg.

We tried to live at Rico's house, but that was the problem. It was his house. The school district he lived in for high school was not the best, and I wanted to graduate with my friends at Graham High. Mama and I moved into an apartment next to the high school. She and Rico stayed together as a couple by living in separate houses.

High school days were the best times at Clearwater Beach. If you skipped school on a sunny day, you could find yourself at Pier 60. You never skipped school on a rainy day.

"Sunshine for miles"! That's what we called it amongst friends, while in school to let them know we were skipping and going to the Pier. It was our code phrase. Some teachers caught on and joked, "You can plan your 'sunshine for miles' another time; we have a test this week." Those were usually the cool teachers, the young teachers. We would often see them at the pier on the weekends.

A bathing suit and flip-flops were all we needed. Cash was how we paid for everything. I always kept money in my bathing suit top. Besides, I only needed enough to buy a burger and fries. We spent time on the beach, walking along the coast and socializing with friends from neighboring schools. As kids, we used to gather at the skating rink. It wasn't until high school we realized they had separated us based on our neighborhood school districts. It was always good to see our classmates from the past. The Pier was where we could come together and reminisce about the good times. My friends from Graham High School were all from the north side of Carroll Pines.

Through the years, Carroll Pines had changed. We lived in the country when I was growing up. There was agriculture on both sides of the streets. Orange groves and cow pastures were all you would see for miles. Ranch-style homes and trailers were scattered near lakes or ponds on spacious properties. When I passed through Carroll Pines, it brought back memories of places where I used to ride Baby. Most houses and trailers were gone or run-down, and large, beautiful farm-style homes were in their place. Housing developments were building up with long driveways filled with multiple cars. You could barely see the lakes or the ponds anymore. No one water skied or swam in these lakes. The alligators have called them their own.

I always enjoyed my morning walks through the complex to school. I crossed the street and navigated through office buildings, reaching the main highway. North Dale Mabry Highway was usually not busy at this time in the morning. There was a crosswalk they'd finally added for those who lived in the neighborhood. If I left our apartment early, I could beat the traffic caused by the buses. The weather was nice in October. It was still warm but not as humid as those summer days. The rainy season had slowed, and the gray clouds now covered the sky.

I was excited about the new school year. It had been over a month since school started, and I was in the groove of my schedule. I was a senior, and I walked the halls with confidence. I remember what Mama said: *keep your shoulders back, your head held high and walk those halls like you belong.* She was right. That small act gave me a boost of confidence and attitude to help me through my days. I would never tell her that, of course.

I got to school early on most days. My friends hung out at "the wall" every morning while we waited for each other to arrive.

Leslie was always late. She and I became close friends during our freshman year. I had tried to get her to pick me up in the mornings, but on top of being late, she once forgot me. Although on a rainy day, she would drop me off after school. Her parents gave her a 1972 Malibu convertible on her 17th birthday.

"One day, I want to drive a convertible to the beach. I'll have all my friends in the car, and we will whistle to all the boys while we drive the streets on Clearwater beach," Leslie bragged.

"I am not whistling at boys. They should whistle at us."

We both laughed as we daydreamed of cruising in her convertible. The school bell rang and Leslie yelled, "Meet you at lunch," and we walked our separate ways. Leslie's parents had strict rules for car passengers. Their rule was that she would not have any passengers in her first year of having her license. She was a month away when her dad gave in.

It was Saturday morning when Leslie called. "Get your bathing suit on. I'm on my way to pick you up!"

She repeated her father's words, "Only Vivian can be in the car. I'll take the keys if you have anyone else riding along."

Fifteen minutes later, she was at my house, and we were cruising to the beach in a convertible with the sounds of Tom Petty and the volume on high.

From my home to Clearwater Beach was almost one hour. We stopped at Burger Bills, ate on the drive, and had our feet in the sand by 12:30. Parking was the worst part about going to Clearwater. The $5 parking spots were usually gone by morning. We got lucky as we pulled in and noticed a few military men walking around. They were physically in better shape than any high school boys we saw here.

"There are a lot of military men in bathing suits today; there must be something going on."

We walked to the beach and found a perfect spot near the pier. Leslie had an aggressive side to her, something I'd always admired. She walked over to the men we had seen in the parking lot.

"Are you in the military?" she asked.

"Yeah, how did you know?" the tall, handsome guy asked.

"Your haircut gives you away. What are you all doing here? MacDill Air Force Base is back in Tampa," I said.

"We drove from Tampa to the beaches to see pretty girls like you," replied the short blond with muscles.

"We have a few days off before we report back. We're staying at the Surfside Inn. You and your friends can come by later. Room 110."

"Maybe we will," Leslie said as we laid our towels down.

Once I knew they were out of earshot, "What? I am not going to a hotel room with military guys."

"I agree, but let's stay here and see if they invite any other girls."

I leaned in, after counting that there were eight of them.

"This is not looking good. Eight guys and only the two of us in a hotel room."

"Exactly. They're military boys. Which means they can't do anything bad because they must keep a clean government reputation," she said, trying to convince me.

"Leslie, I hate to break the news to you, but anyone in a government job is okay with a bad reputation." We laughed.

We agreed that being with eight men alone, military or not, was not an option. And besides, she needed to return the car by 6:00 tonight. Her dad asked her to call throughout the day to check in. We spent the day meeting with friends from school and walking on the beach. With the Gulf beside us, cool and refreshing, we never stepped further than to our knees.

The Surfside Inn was the local hotel with a Tiki Hut bar serving drinks and outside dining. The pool was our go-to spot whenever we needed to cool off. We didn't take up any patio furniture to avoid bringing attention to ourselves.

"Now we have a room number. So, if they stop us, we can say we're staying in room 110." We ordered some cokes from the Tiki bar and paid the bill for our drinks. We began our walk back to the beach when I heard my name being called.

"Vivi, is that you?" I looked back and noticed the military boys were watching us.

"I don't remember telling them my name," I said.

"They never asked us our names."

One boy stood up and walked toward us. Leslie started talking, but I didn't know what she was saying. I was focused on this gorgeous body walking directly at me.

"I wondered if that was you. Oh wow, Vivi Perez. How have you been?"

With the sun in my eyes, I couldn't see who it was. He looked cute. He was short, stocky, and had no hair. I saw his blue eyes just as he approached my face. *I know you.* My mind was blank at first. It took me a minute to realize it was him.

"Danny? Oh, my gosh. What are you doing here?"

He swooped me into his arms with a huge hug and swung me around. I stood and held his arm while I caught my balance.

He grew up!

"Man, I never thought I would see you again," he said loud for everyone to hear.

"What are you doing here? Don't you live in North Carolina?" I changed my posture, pushed out my chest, hoping I looked my best in this bathing suit.

I should have worn the black one today.

Still in shock, Leslie stood there staring at us. I couldn't stop grinning.

"Do you know this guy?" Leslie leaned toward the table of gorgeous men and asked, "Do you guys know Vivi?"

We scrambled to find chairs around the table while Danny shared our history.

I interrupted, "I thought you were in North Carolina?"

"I was. After graduation, I joined the Air Force. I was off to basic training and went to Texas for my AIT training. I hoped to stay at Lackland Air Force Base for my permanent duty station, but they sent me here to MacDill along with all these losers," he said.

Leslie looked at me and asked, "Are you in the Air Force and forgot to tell me?"

We all laughed. I felt embarrassed.

"No. When I lived in North Carolina, Danny and I went to school together. I had a huge crush on him back then." The words came out before I could stop them.

In unison, they all teased, "Woohoo! A crush." We both blushed, and I could not pull my stare from his big blue eyes.

We moved to the pool to cool off, and I wore Danny's hat to keep the sun off my face while he wore sunglasses that kept me from seeing his eyes. As we both treaded water, our conversation continued, telling our stories of the past five years. He shared he would be at MacDill for the next four years, and I shared I was living with my mom and enjoying my senior year.

"We come to Clearwater every weekend if it doesn't rain. If you want to find me, I'll be at Pier 60," I said.

Danny liked that. "Good to know. I can drive an hour to see you."

"Actually, I live closer to MacDill. The base is less than an hour from my house."

Danny's eyes lit up, a smile formed, and those dancing eyebrows gave a bouncing nod. "Oh, really!"

I had missed those eyebrows.

The time flew by as we sat by the pool talking. Leslie got to know Mitchell well. He kept inviting her back to the hotel room, but I told her to stay with me. Danny asked for my phone number and promised to call me soon. He mentioned they would be at the beach tomorrow if we wanted to return. But Leslie knew she could only go to the beach once per weekend. We said our goodbyes at five o'clock and hoped to see them again.

"Maybe next weekend?"

They watched us get into the convertible and drive away, and *I heard one of them whistle!*

DANNY

At first, we spent each day together after work and school. I was loving this time with him. I could not get enough of his attention. Mama continued going to Rico's house and left the car with me during the week. Rico would take her to work.

"Since you're a senior now, you can drive to school," she said.

I would leave school, drive to the coffee shop, or meet Danny at a restaurant for dinner. The distance from my home in North Tampa to the base in South Tampa was less than an hour's drive. The commute sometimes was longer, depending on the steady traffic along Dale Mabry Highway.

"It would make it easier for us to spend time together if we had an apartment," he said. He was living on base with five other men and never had privacy. I knew I could never bring him to stay overnight at our apartment. Mama would sometimes come home early on the weekends. I had invited Danny to meet Mama, but he said, "I have never been good with parents."

We discussed marriage and children. He repeatedly stated, "I have no plans to marry. I hope you feel the same way. My parents married after dating for four years and felt they would be together forever. But, once they reached 20 years of marriage, they were both in their forties and went their separate ways. It crushed me. I vowed to myself that I would never get married."

"I can agree if I'm being honest. Today, people perceive marriage differently than in our parents' generation. I agree that love doesn't always have to be sealed with a marriage certificate to be long-lasting," I said.

I said it, but I wasn't sure I believed it.

We continued our evenings together after he got off work and spent most of the weekend days and nights together. Danny found a reasonable rate at a hotel on the base. We started spending more time there. The room had a full kitchen, so we bought groceries and cooked meals together. I realized a few things were happening, but I found myself afraid to share my feelings or thoughts with Danny. Would he run away if I told him I want to be in a committed relationship and could see myself doing this forever? He told me things I liked to hear while lying in bed.

"I could live with a girl, just not be married," he said.

"Any girl or me?"

He never gave me a straightforward answer; instead, he would turn the time into fun—tickling and rolling around until we were heated again.

Then there were those nights that he would open up to me and share intimate feelings and thoughts. As I drove home, I felt confused, wondering why I sensed the tension between us. I noticed a pattern was forming. We would meet during the weekend, usually on Friday afternoons. Danny would call me to give me the room number and time.

"At the Surfside or the Base Hotel?" I asked.

"On Fridays, let's meet at the Surfside Inn on the beach. During the week, let's meet at the Base Hotel."

It became a routine of how I would spend my weekdays awaiting his call. My weekends became all about him. I stopped spending time with family and friends, and our time together was affecting my schoolwork.

I planned to leave by 11 o'clock on Sunday nights, but we ended up staying in bed, rolling around. We would fall asleep and wake up at 3 am for me to drive home. I had little sleep and classes in the morning. Danny sensed something was wrong after a few months of this routine.

"You know I am starting college next fall?" I said.

During this time, Danny shared his plans with me as well. "Vivi, I have loved spending this time with you these past few months. I feel we have become so close in such a short time. At Christmas, I'll go home for two weeks. This year will be busy; I report back in January and then leave for California for additional training. So, I won't be back here until April. In June, I leave for another duty outside of the country. It would be best if you didn't wait for me. You have your life here with your friends at school, and I have my life in the Air Force, with plans to further myself, too," he said.

Shock overwhelmed me. I stood there listening and could not help but cry. Realizing my feelings, I came to understand that I was falling in love and simultaneously having my heart shattered. We held each other as my words muffled into his shoulder.

"Why does it feel we are always getting together at the wrong time in our lives?"

Our last weekend was special; we stayed inside all day and night Saturday, making love, holding one another, and watching back-to-back rom-com movies. I knew the weekend was ending, but I hoped for another chance the next day.

In the morning, I began, "You know I was thinking, since we both will be so busy these next few months, let's focus on our jobs and school until you return next summer. Can we reunite and continue from where we left off?"

He had already thought this through.

"Vivi, I don't want to be exclusive to anyone. I love you but cannot focus on you while I am in training," he said with such conviction. I knew there was no changing his mind.

"So, you're saying that I'm a distraction? Well, that's a problem you can overcome."

But he didn't care to hear that.

"No. This is what I want for myself. I cannot have my mind on you while I am in a new city over the next four to six months and can't promise I won't meet new people," he said.

And I realized he was breaking up with me so he wouldn't feel bad when he met someone new.

"I got it, loud and clear!"

Whether I was overreacting, I didn't care. As I gathered my things, I hurriedly shoved them into my bag, feeling pressured and determined to get out of the room.

I raised my voice. "You should know I don't want to marry or have children. But I was willing to wait for you. You can't be sure you won't change your mind one day!"

"I'm sorry, Vivi. It's just not what I want."

I went to the car and threw my things in the trunk. He didn't come outside. I saw him pull back the curtains and look out the window. He was wiping tears away, too. I sat in the car for a few minutes, crying, hoping that he would come out and stop me, but he didn't. While I drove home, every song was a love song, and the tears kept coming.

"Why are you home early?" Mama asked.

"I don't want to talk about it. We broke up. Danny leaves next week and doesn't want me to wait for him," I said.

Over the next few days, it was difficult not to call him. I just reminded myself that he didn't want to be with me. Calling him would make me look weak and needy. Liv came over and told me what she had learned from marrying too young.

"Don't make yourself look desperate. After Billy and I divorced, it took all I had not to call him and beg him to take me back. But I am glad that I didn't. I promise the pain will go away."

Part Six

Young Adult

SOMETHING WAS MISSING

The holidays had come and gone. The New Year was here. I was with Mama and Liv when they told me about their New Year's night dancing. Mama had fallen while on the dance floor and broken her arm. They took her to the hospital, and a cast was placed.

"And with all the excitement of the New Year and Mama falling, I didn't notice that my period started and leaked through my dress," Liv shared her story.

We all started laughing. It was then that I realized.

"Oh, my God. I've not had a period since …" I stopped and thought about it. And then I realized, "… since October?"

They both stopped laughing, and in shock, they looked at me and laughed again. I didn't know whether to laugh with them or start crying.

"Vivian, are you sure? You forgot December's period? You may have forgotten you had it, since you've been busy with the holidays and exams?" Mama said.

I can't believe this is happening.

I shook my head. "No. No. I haven't had a period. I had a feeling something was wrong."

They stopped laughing.

"You're serious? Let's go to the clinic on Monday. They'll give you a pregnancy test to confirm. You've had a lot of stress this past month. You can miss a period if you have too much stress. Right Mama?" Liv said.

"Ay, si. You can miss a period with too much stress," Mama agreed.

"But this would be TWO PERIODS. Is that normal, Liv?" I shouted, standing up to get out of the room. I began pacing. Sure, I was more tired than usual and would sleep more on the weekends. But I did well on my exams the last week of school before winter break. I finished the semester strong. I was missing Danny, sure. It came to a point where I realized we would be better off apart. I considered my time with him a "second chance" to finish what we started in North Carolina. Not everyone gets the chance to 'redo' a relationship.

On Monday, I'd visit the clinic.

On Valentine's Day, I was hoping to hear from Danny. In my imagination, he would come to my apartment with flowers and scoop me up in his arms. *I have our baby growing inside me*. And he would say, *Let's get married and raise him together*.

But when the doorbell rang, and I opened it, it was Leslie.

"Let's go. Get dressed and do something with your hair. We're meeting Mitchell and some friends of his at a club near the base," she said. "And no, Danny will not be there. I don't think Mitchell and Danny hang out anymore since Danny is in the Unit going to Spain next week. Oh my God, you knew that, right?"

"Yes, I know."

She was rushing through my closet and pulling out different tops with skirts.

"We need to hurry; do something with your hair and put on some makeup. Mitchell is meeting us in one hour. You know how bad traffic can get near the base."

She stopped to take a breath and realized I was not moving.

"Why aren't you hurrying?"

"Hey Leslie, I'm pregnant!"

She stopped going through my closet, spun, and looked up and down at my body.

"Oh, my God. Well, that explains the weight gain on your face. Sorry, but it's true. Whose is it? Is it Danny's?"

I lied.

"No. We broke up months ago. The person I had a one-night

stand with now wants nothing to do with me. He's not from around here," I said.

"Are you keeping it?"

"Yes, of course. My mom and Liv will help me. I plan to finish school and go to college part time. It'll be fine," I lied again. "Look, I get it. It's Saturday night, and you need someone to party with. But I am not that girl. The thought of alcohol and staying up past midnight dancing makes me nauseous. Those days are over for me. Go, have fun, but my belly and I are staying in."

Leslie grabbed her bag and walked towards the door.

"If I were not in such a rush, I would drag you out of here. We should get together and hang out. I'll call you," she said.

I was even more tired after she left. Watching her rush around the closet with all her adrenaline made me jealous. I used to have that frenzy for fun. But those days were gone. I called Mama to see what she was doing on a Saturday night.

"Are you getting ready to go dancing?"

"Unfortunately, not tonight. Rico and I invited some friends over to play Canasta. I made some rice and Picadillo if you want to come over."

She could hear the loneliness in my voice.

"Who are you having over?" I asked.

"You know Alice and Dieter from work? You met them at the picnic a few years ago."

"Oh yeah, they have a son Liv's age?"

I remembered him because Liv was making out with him behind the baseball dugout one year.

"We can't have over four players for Canasta, but I still want you to come for dinner. I have other games we can all play together," Mama said.

My stomach was growling with hunger.

"I will come by for a little while. Picadillo and rice sound delicious. I won't stay for the games, but I'll drive over. I'll see you then."

And Mama was happy with that. I was glad I didn't have to cook.

I didn't realize being pregnant would be more than just growing a person in my belly. But my hips changed, my boobs were bigger and sore. My hands were swollen, and I could no longer wear rings on every finger. But the one thing that I noticed most about being pregnant was that my mood changed.

A commercial featuring baby pandas would move me to tears or a young fawn taking its first steps. Mama would call and ask if I wanted to join them for dinner, and I would respond rudely. After a few days passed, she and Liv would share how the two of them went to dinner, leaving me to feel left out.

"Why didn't I go with you to dinner?"

"I don't know. We asked you, and you said you had other things to do."

It was then that Mama noticed through my tears that I was dealing with more than just pregnancy.

"Of course, this is going to happen. Not only is your body changing, but your mind is, too."

I felt exhausted and would have been content to stay in my room and cry all day.

"Why don't you go to counseling?" Mama suggested.

She explained how they would offer the right tools for me to use to better my mind and body.

"Especially while you have this baby growing inside you."

I began going to therapy once a week after school. I replaced that extra time from not being with Danny; it had played on my emotions. Although right now I had time to myself, soon all that would change.

GREEN WITH ENVY

I remained in school until spring break. I graduated high school as a homeschool student, completing all the classwork. Mama had talked with one of her friends, a schoolteacher, and she had me over to monitor while I took the final exams. I did that over one weekend, and by May, I was done. Mama went to the school the week after my birthday and collected my diploma. I never had the ceremonial walk across the stage like everyone else. That bothered me the most.

My belly had grown, and my small, thin body looked like I had a basketball underneath my shirt. I had a few names picked out. Both Mama and Liv kept choosing girl names, and I kept choosing boy names. Although gender didn't matter to me, the idea of a little boy made me smile. I realized things were getting real. This was happening faster than I was prepared for. We drove to Paddock Mall to go baby shopping on a Saturday. We bought a few things for the day of delivery. Rico gave me money to buy a crib.

"Green or yellow is neutral for baby colors," Liv said.

As soon as we got home, I spotted Rico moving a few of his things into the apartment.

"Your mother and I feel it would be best if we spend the last months with you here, until the baby comes," he said.

In my bedroom, we cleared space for the crib and adorned it with plush toys and blankets. It all came together in a soft shade of green.

There were those moments when I got depressed and felt alone. The thought of being eighteen and pregnant made me feel selfish, and I didn't want anyone to know I was having a baby, so that brought on feelings of shame.

This baby came at the worst possible time in my life, I kept thinking. I had plans to attend college and live on campus. My dreams had changed; the worst part was that I had to handle it alone. I couldn't even call Danny and ask for his help because he made it clear that this was not what he wanted. And then I felt a "twitch" along my stomach. I lifted my shirt and saw an arm or a foot rolling across my belly. It hurt, but in a good way. I placed my hand over the arm/foot and rubbed it.

Hey there, buddy. We are going to be okay. I may not know what I am doing, but we can figure it out together. And I went to the refrigerator and devoured two chocolate popsicles. I was so glad Mama bought those for me, for us.

FREDDY

He was born on July 6th. I was glad he wasn't born on the Fourth of July, as Mama had hoped.
No one other than my family saw my belly grow and my ankles bloat. I was always sick and tired at the beginning of the pregnancy. I could not believe women did this multiple times. On the day he was born, the nurse put him in my arms. I had no pain. None of that mattered.

Danny came back from his tour in June, then left again in early July, just a few weeks later. So, I knew he had not discovered Freddy. I was keeping my secret to myself. I made it clear to Mama and Liv that I would raise Freddy on my own, without his presence. Knowing his reluctance to start a family, they stood by me and encouraged me to make the choice that felt right for me.

His name was Frederick Joseph Perez. He and I shared the same last name. I decided that someday, if I got married and my last name changed, then that was when his name would change, too.

I called him Freddy. His dark hair and gray eyes, which eventually turned hazel, were just like mine.

"Ay sweet Frederico. His good sleep and eating habits make things easier for a young mother. You don't realize how good he is," Mama said.

Once I discovered I was pregnant, I prayed God would help me raise him because I knew I could not depend on his father to help us. I created a story, a lie I had to live. I was so caught up in it I completely forgot about Freddy being affected. One day he would grow up and want to know more, but I didn't care about anything but myself and the decision that I had made. He was my son. I was the mother. It was my body, and I would be responsible for the decisions that I made for us. And I told myself this story over and over.

I knew who the father was, but I never gave him the chance to change his mind. At this age, I never wanted to be married or raise my son with anyone else. Now that he was here, I'd be a wonderful mom.

The phone rang. "Hello?"

"Hey, stranger." It was Danny. "I am heading back to MacDill this week. Do you want to go to dinner?"

"Oh, Danny. It's good to hear from you. I am not sure if going to dinner is a good idea," I said, with a steady voice.

"Relax, it's just dinner. Can't two friends have a nice dinner together?" I could hear his smirk through the line.

A part of me wanted to answer yes; I had missed him, and there was so much to tell him. "Sure, when?"

I called Mama.

"Hello. Would you be available to watch Freddy Saturday night?"

I lied and told her that Carmen and Shannon wanted to meet for dinner. Mama was happy that we were spending time together again. It was true, Shannon *was* back in town. She had moved back to live with her mom after graduating from high school. We only spoke once on the phone, though.

I gave Danny a call back. I wasn't ready to explain all the baby furniture and toys. We agreed to have an early dinner and met at an Italian restaurant near the base.

It was nice seeing him again. He shared stories of everywhere he had been. He asked me about school and then he invited me back to his place on base. While I drove and followed behind him, I realized we were going towards the Base Hotel, and I smiled, aware of his intentions to be together. I felt the same way.

We spent the next three hours making love and holding each other. He continued to lie to me, too. He said things that every girl wanted to hear.

"I have missed you. I think about you. We should get back together."

I stopped him there. Things were different for me now. Having

Freddy made my perspective of Danny change. I didn't need him anymore to make me feel love and longing. Although I allowed him to kiss and love me without objection, reconciling our relationship was where I drew the line.

"Danny, I enjoyed this time with you. But I cannot put my heart back into this again."

He agreed. "Let's have a fun-time-friendship," he said.

It was difficult for me not to laugh. "I can do that. I can engage in fun activities with you without worrying about any negative consequences."

"Wow! You've changed during the holidays. You were upset about us, but now you're more understanding."

"No. I'm just mature and want more for myself. I only came here for the same thing you did, no offense."

There, I said it. Without saying *it*.

We rolled around one more time. Being free and laughing with him felt good. I knew I was telling him exactly what he wanted to hear, but somehow, this time, I felt in control.

"Where are you going? It's not morning yet. We have the room until tomorrow." He leaned in and watched me from the bed as I dressed.

I knelt down, kissed him goodbye, and breathed, "Until next time."

"Is there going to be a next time?" he asked with his eyes glued on me.

I walked away and gave him a wink as I shut the door. *Oh yes. I want more.*

That became the first of many "fun-time friends" moments we shared. He would call when he was in town or missing me. During a rushed phone call, he blurted out, "Room 210, 7 pm tonight. Let's meet." I started getting random messages with a room number and the time. He later confessed he was too busy to call and talk but would think of me whenever he saw a pay phone. I would create a lie that I was spending time with friends and ask Mama to watch Freddy, then I would drive and meet him in the hotel room. We would have fun. After a few hours, I would leave. I loved it.

I loved the control I had over this time with him. The

commitment was no longer necessary for me. I just had fun.
And that gave me a thrill, even more!

Part Seven

Mature

August

I had hoped to start college full time, but caring for a baby was also a full-time job. I couldn't afford to do both. Mama and Rico were ready to move in together, and I couldn't afford that big apartment on my own.

A year had passed since Freddy was born, and I decided I needed to do more with myself. I applied for various jobs but hadn't heard back after a few weeks. I was grateful when Credential Services emailed me to request an interview. When I got home from the interview, I received a phone call with an offer for the position. I was ecstatic! Freddy had turned one that summer, and I had changed my life.

"Ay, Vivian, now that you have a job, you don't need me here. Rico and I are ready to live together again," she said.

"I agree, Mama. Now that you don't have a teenager to raise, you can enjoy each other's time. Thank you for sacrificing these past few years to live with me. I understand."

"No sacrifice. You are my baby; I know you would do the same for your son, too," she said.

I enrolled Freddy into a daycare near work and found a studio apartment nearby. Mama and Rico helped with the deposit and said they would watch Freddy when I needed time alone. They transferred the car to me, and I moved to an apartment that was less than a 10-minute drive from their place.

Mama retired that summer. She and Rico took time to travel. I was glad for them both. She deserved this. I felt a sense of happiness as I started working and was finally able to envision my future. I called Danny because I wanted to share my news.

"Hey there, good-time friend," he said.

"Fun-time friend, not good time," I said.

"Fun-time is a good time." We laughed.

"So, what are you doing tonight?" he asked.

"I just wanted to let you know I found a full-time job and I have an apartment."

"What about college? How will you manage school and work?"

"Well, that was an issue I had to choose, and I chose work. My mom moved in with Rico, and I moved out alone."

That's when I told him.

"Well, I am not moving out on my own. I have a roommate; his name is Freddy. He's my son," I winced.

Danny was silent for a few seconds.

"What? Did you say your son?"

"Yes, I have a son." I panicked and started lying once again.

"Don't worry, he's not yours. I met someone shortly after we broke up, and he took off when he found out I was pregnant. He has no desire to be part of Freddy's life. My mom and Rico have been helping me take care of him, and now that I am working full time, I got us an apartment." I stopped talking.

"That sounds great. Next time, I can come by and meet Fred."

"Yeah, that would be great. And his name is Freddy," I said.

Several months passed before I heard from Danny again. I was doing great at my new job. Freddy and I had a routine. I would drop him at daycare before work and Mama would pick him up and take him back to her house. I would pick him up from Mama's after work and have dinner with them. Everyone learned I had a baby. My phone stopped ringing for a while. Leslie called to check on me and asked about Freddy. When I invited her to meet him or go to the beach together, she had excuses. She moved on, and so did I.

Raising a baby was challenging and often lonely. It became difficult without someone to bounce ideas off of, help change diapers or put him to sleep when he woke up at three in the morning. I could not imagine my life without him, but I wished I had someone in my life, too.

I called Danny.

"You want to come over and see my new place?"

He sounded distant. "Hey, not sure if today is good for me. The guys and I have some things we are doing tonight. Maybe another night?"

"No worries. Let me know when you're available. I can see if Mama can watch Freddy another time. Good night." And I hung up.

I had just put Freddy in the bath when the phone rang.

"It looks like the guys are going to go without me. What time can I come over?"

"Oh, okay. Let me drop Freddy off at my mom's place, and I should return home by 7:30. I'll text you my address."

I was giddy and excited to finish bath time with Freddy. When I returned from Mama's house, I ordered takeout to be delivered, thinking we could share a meal in my apartment. Once out of the shower, I blow-dried and styled my hair into gentle waves. I put on a light blue sundress with spaghetti straps, and the skirt was short enough that it showed my tanned legs. Despite a small apartment and baby toys scattered everywhere, I cleaned up as much as possible. But I also wanted him to know that I had a son. I didn't want to keep hiding my sweet boy.

The doorbell rang, and I peeked out the hole to see the delivery guy. It was 7:40; delivery was on time. Danny was not.

Not until the clock struck eight did I allow myself to sit down and enjoy my long-awaited dinner. At 8:15, I called him. He didn't answer. I stored the leftovers and relaxed on the couch as I scrolled through the channels. I came across a classic love story and enjoyed the night alone watching the movie *Somewhere in Time*.

I Got a Name

One day, I was listening to the radio while driving. They were playing songs from the past.

Music always gave me comfort. And there were times when it brought back memories, especially songs from Croce's greatest hits. Singing along, I drove down Willowdale Road. I hoped to see Carmen or someone in the neighborhood to stop and talk to. Even though I enjoyed the memories this street brought back, my past haunted me.

After an awful night of struggling to fall asleep, I woke up filled with anxiety. When I shared this with Mama, she knew that I had stopped seeing the therapist after I had Freddy.

"You need to go back to therapy."

She was right. I had only stopped because I'd believed I had control over the pain and confusion I was feeling over Danny.

But that time during my therapy sessions, I learned *that the power I'd lost as a child could determine the power I allowed someone to take as an adult.* I had never realized the two were connected.

I knew I did not kill Daddy. I understood that cancer took care of that for me. It was difficult to counsel away stewing anger and pain. The most powerful thing I learned from therapy was to have forgiveness. Forgiving someone didn't imply acceptance of their actions. To forgive someone was not for them; it was to release me from anger and hate. It allowed me to move on and be a better person. But the more I went to counseling, the more I hated him. It was as though I was keeping the story alive and making it harder to forget.

What made me give so much power to someone no longer alive? Why was I allowing him to haunt me from the grave? Why didn't I let him stay dead and be at peace? I could not change him, but I could change myself. My decision was to forgive. I realized my dad was once a child who must have had a terrible adult in his life. He grew up in a time when society expected women and children to be silent.

Through the years, I have learned that love, kindness, and respect live within me. I was unsure if any of that was from him, but I knew it was because of him I was better and stronger.

... so life won't pass me by. I got a name.

And for the first time, I wept. I was nineteen.

Part Eight

Adulting

FREECE

It had been a few months since I started working at Credential Services. My shift started at 7:00 in the morning. When I arrived at 6:50, I noticed a black truck was already there. When I left work at 4:30, the black truck would be gone. Like a magnet, it drew my eyes to the parking lot, checking for the truck's presence. I played this game every morning by myself. *Will the truck be there? Did I arrive first?*

One of my first memories of him was before I knew his name. The "big black truck" turned the corner into the parking lot. I felt it creeping slowly along the back row. It was the sound of his truck that caught my attention. The truck squeaked as it slowly bounced over the speed bumps, arriving at work like a seasoned pro. The truck knew precisely where to go, straight to its parking space as if it were driving itself. I had seen that black truck in that same space every day. He'd park in the farthest spot, last row, back corner. The black truck was old and faded because of sun damage. The oxidation spots showed its age and still it wore its shiny accessories. A custom license plate that said BOLT5 and a silver frame with the words Home of the New York Yankees written around the border of his Florida license plate.

Wanting to know who the driver was, I started arriving earlier than the black truck. It felt like a magnetic force, a curse, pulling me to uncover the identity of the person behind the wheel of this black truck. Through my rearview mirror, I had a clear view of him, the driver. I watched him get out of his truck, leaving the door open while he took off his sunglasses and leaned over. He reached to get his backpack. Only his head was visible through the door's window. Stepping back, he closed the door, careful not to slam it as I would have expected. He walked away from the truck, swinging the backpack over his shoulder, and clicking the key remote. The truck responded with a horn and a beep.

Wow! Fancy car alarm.

In one glance, I noticed his hair, shirt, jeans, and boots. Today, he was wearing a white short-sleeve shirt with a collar. He wore the shirt untucked, hanging just above his butt. He was wearing faded blue jeans snug to his legs and brown construction boots. His hair was a mix of brown and light brown, nicely trimmed over the ears, and I could tell he wore hair products—the wet look but not wet, messy but not messy. From now on, I would consider this style as *sexy hair*.

After dropping Freddy off at the daycare, I arrived early, which allowed me some reading time. I began parking in the same spot, too—the second-to-last row at the second parking space to the end. His truck was directly behind me. It was a bold move, I knew. But I decided this would be "my game". I'd arrive early to see him enter the parking lot and check his appearance.

I continued this game for no other reason, but because he was nice to look at.

All I knew about the truck driver was his interest in hockey and the Yankees.

And he was very sexy.

I knew nothing about hockey, but I knew plenty about baseball. All those years of watching baseball with Daddy had finally paid off. I could use that information to strike up some small talk.

So, I see you like the Yankees; I'm a Tampa Bay Rays fan. Maybe we should go to a game together and watch the Rays beat the Yankees?

One day, I'd have the courage to say it. We had that in common!

I would usually sit at my desk during lunchtime and catch up on my reading. Susannah came over when she saw my book, *The Birds and*

the Beeswax.

"I just finished the third book in that series. It gets better. Let me know if you want to borrow the rest of the series. Rita and I walk on the track during our breaks for some exercise and have lunch in the courtyard. Would you like to join us?" she asked.

We were fortunate to work at such a high-scale location. The building offered a running track on the first floor, surrounding the gym that overlooked the parking lot. In the restrooms were lockers and showers. It always surprised me to see people showering at work.

We took advantage of the cooler months by having our lunch break outdoors. Umbrella-shaded picnic tables were scattered throughout the courtyard. Unfortunately, in the summer, we were forced to eat in the breakroom because of the unbearable heat and humidity.

Susannah and Rita would talk about their home life, and I enjoyed sharing about Danny, even though we weren't officially dating. How we would spend our weekends at the beach walking, shopping, and meeting for dinner during the week.

They would ask, "Are you meeting Danny tonight?" They eventually stopped asking about Danny when I shared he had not yet met my family or Freddy. It was then that I realized how our relationship must look from their perspective.

I felt comfortable enough to ask after a few weeks of walking with them. "I wonder who drives that black truck; it's always in the same spot."

"That's Freece's truck," Susannah said.

She answered so quickly.

"Did you say his name is Reece?"

Raising her voice. "No. It's Freece. Freece Miles. He's a nice guy."

That's it? That's all she's going to say. I needed more.

There was nothing I could say to get her to tell me more without giving her the suspicion that I was interested. I shouldn't have shared my personal life, but secretly, I was smiling.

His name was Freece. What a cool name. Freece Miles, the sexy guy who drives the black truck!

THE BIRDS AND THE BEESWAX

This was such a good book, and I was excited to move on to the next in the series. The main character was attractive because I imagined him looking like Freece. I stayed distracted between reading and looking for the black truck.

I loved the sunny days when Freece wore his sunglasses.

What makes a man in sunglasses so appealing?

I shifted in my seat, sitting upright, when I saw him open the truck door. His truck was so dirty, and he was so clean.

All right! Here we go ...

Each day I was obsessed with watching him as he repeated the same routine: he'd put away his sunglasses, grabbed his backpack, stepped back, and closed the door. As he walked away, he clicked the remote key, and the alarm barked and beeped. His walk was more like a glide, and his posture showed confidence. That was what I noticed that day: he had excellent posture. Although he didn't look taller than five feet ten inches, he was still taller than me.

Today's ensemble was a collared black shirt, faded jeans, and boots; his hair was still a sexy mess. I finally decided that I was ready to approach him and talk. I didn't know what I would say, but it was time. I needed him to notice me. *What can go wrong? Can we be friends? Everyone could use a friend.*

That day, during our walk, Susannah and Rita reminded me that the company was covering our lunch. During the holidays, they had a week where they celebrated the employees by providing lunch. They announced over the intercom: *Good morning, team! Please wait until your department has been called before going to the breakroom.*

It was noon when my team was called for lunch. A long line had started, and as I approached the food tables, I noticed my supervisor was one of those who was serving the meals.

"Vivian, which pizza would you like - cheese, meat, or vegetable? Choose two slices, and we have salad, ice cream, and a can of soda," Phyllis said.

And there he was, standing beside Phyllis; they were talking and laughing. He looked right at me and smiled while adding a salad to my plate. And then he spoke to me.

"Vivian? Would you like ranch or blue cheese dressing?"

It was as though everyone in the room was silent. His voice was only a whisper as he said my name. *"Vivian."*

I picked up on his accent and noticed his deep voice.

"I'll take everything from the branch. I mean ranch, I'll have ranch dressing," I stammered.

Susannah laughed. "I'll take the branch as well."

I felt completely humiliated and turned bright red from embarrassment. Phyllis made her way to our table as we sat and listened to the announcements of those who received awards for Employee Week.

The chatter of everyone made it difficult to hear the speaker as they announced the top ten employees who had *gone above and beyond* over the past year! One by one, the employee would move to the microphone and accept the plaque, with only a simple *thank you* spoken. The crowd would give applause as each person moved forward.

I continued eating while keeping one eye on his movements.

"And we would like to recognize one person as Credential's Employee of the Year, to Freece Miles. He oversaw the project that his department had been working on ..." She continued speaking as I watched him stand and move to accept his award.

As though I had known him, I began clapping with such pride. I barely knew his name, and I gave applause as though my best friend had just won an Emmy Award!

He accepted the award and uttered, "Thank you" into the microphone, and quickly rushed away.

Phyllis was clapping and leaned in towards us. "He's so shy. He hates having to get up in front of everyone."

I was the only one at my table paying attention to Phyllis.

"Were you here during Freece's long-haired days? Remember his hair was past his butt? I remember he came in and had the warehouse guys shave his head. He donated all his hair to children's cancer. He is such a good guy. I can't believe he's never been married or has a girlfriend," Phyllis exclaimed. And then she added, "And no, he's not gay. He's simply a guy who's taking his time."

And my heart skipped another beat.

Finally, someone had more information.

I dropped Freddy off early. I'd been arriving late a few days and had missed seeing Freece show up. I noticed that his black truck was still not there. Almost finished with this book, just one chapter remaining out of 500 pages, and I was determined to finish before I entered the office. When I glanced at the clock, it was just 6:30. *I can finish this book within 15 minutes and still have time to see him arrive.*

I heard a door shut and people talking and walking past my car. *I know it isn't him; he drives alone to work.* I continued reading.

Suddenly, I stopped and looked up, only to realize I had two pages left. I saw the black truck in my rearview mirror. *Wait! That can't be him. It's too early. It was 6:56. Holy crap! I was going to be late and that door I heard shut was him.*

With my keys, purse, book, and lunch bag in hand, I opened the door. I moved my legs to step out and got pulled back inside. I still had my seatbelt on! *Oh my gosh!*

I dropped everything back in the seat to unfasten my belt and try again. I was definitely going to be late. Walking as fast as I could without running, I was careful not to trip, on the day I wore pumps. *Don't run. Don't trip. Don't talk to yourself. Whoever is watching from the windows will see you.* I reached the time clock and found a line of people.

As I waited, I daydreamed … *Freece walks straight over to me. He leans towards my ear and whispers, "Hello Vivian, don't worry, you aren't late." He looked deep into my eyes, and still I can't make out their color.*

And there he was, he was assisting with the installation of a new time clock. I approached him as he held the door for the employees. Rushing up the stairs wearing heels caused me to trip and fall on the steps. Freece leaned down and offered his hand towards me as we locked eyes. What felt like an eternity was only a brief second. But enough time to notice. His eyes *were blue.*

The clouds were hiding the sun today, so we ate outside. They added more tables to the courtyard, each with a bright turquoise umbrella. My favorite all-time lunch was a ham sandwich with provolone cheese, plain potato chips, and a few red grapes left over from the morning. I preferred a lot of ice in my cup and always drank with a straw.

While Susannah was holding our table, I stepped away to the ice and vending machine for a soda. I saw Freece walking through the courtyard. The windows allowed me to watch him without being seen. He stopped to talk to Susannah, which caused me some jealousy of not being present. Then I saw him walk away and head inside, towards me. I put my head down and hurried past him as though I didn't notice that he was heading in my direction.

"Hey there."

I don't know what to do.

"Oh hey," I mumbled in a rush, and kept walking.

I may have been giving off the wrong vibe. Shannon used to tell me that boys liked it when you gave them a challenge, played hard to get, or seemed uninterested. *If they keep trying more than once, they genuinely like you. If they give up after the first try, let them go. They only want one thing.*

Our office space held over sixty cubicles, all working amongst the noise and steady rhythm to meet the quota. Computers hummed and printers chattered constantly at each station. I noticed the ink was out in my printer and caused my data sheets to show blank pages.

"Where do I get an ink cartridge for my printer?" I asked.

"Send the IT department a chat about what you need," Phyllis responded.

I saw on my chat list the names of those in the IT to contact when computer issues occur. There it was: Fmiles@it. I messaged Fmiles@it, pretending I didn't recognize the name.

Vperez@billing: Hello, I am having trouble with my printer. My data sheets are printed with no ink. Can you assist?

Fmiles@it: Hello, do you know what type of printer you have?

Vperez@billing: HP 420Z

I cleaned up my desk and waited. He never showed. Instead, he sent one of his coworkers.

Keep the Faith

It was 6:39 in the morning, and I was ready. I'd completed book two. My mission that day was not to begin the next book until I had talked to him. I left early to drop Freddy at daycare, stopped by the coffee shop, and arrived on time. I was in my parking space, ready. The space behind me was his, but it was empty, so I knew he hadn't arrived. I thought of a few things I could bring up for conversation, and this time, I took off my seatbelt. My purse was on my shoulder, and my lunch bag and keys were in my hand. I was ready!

There it was! The sound of his truck bouncing over the speed bumps. I glanced to see if it was him.

It was!

He pulled up behind me and, per the routine, stepped out, put his sunglasses away, grabbed his backpack, closed the door, and clicked the remote. He walked past my driver's door, and with all my excitement, I almost opened the door before him. But I waited until he passed. Nervously, I stepped out and slammed the door; I clicked my remote and kept my pace behind him.

Slow down, don't walk so fast, not too close, but don't get too far away.

I have just a few minutes to speak. Just us two out here. I shouted, "Hey, Freece, I heard you used to have long hair?"

You could have asked about baseball or hockey. You could have thanked him for sending over one of his employees yesterday to fix the printer. Long hair?

He stopped walking and turned around. *Oh my God, here we go.*

He had a smile that made his blue eyes gleam. He had a mouth full of teeth. Beautiful teeth.

"Where did you hear about that?" he said.

"Oh wow, you have an accent. Where are you from?" I asked. *My mouth was talking too fast.*

"No, I don't have an accent. I'm from New York. And where did you hear about me having long hair?"

We started walking. Climbing four steps to the door, I suddenly realized my employee badge was not out. I panicked. He swiped his badge, opened the door, and held it for me to enter. Once inside, I was standing at the time clock, searching with one hand in my purse for my badge. I pulled it out; he pushed the button that read TIME IN, and I swiped my badge.

"Phyllis told us you had long hair and shaved it to donate it to children's cancer," I said.

He walked away. "Yeah, I had to shave it because too many people thought I was looking like Jon Bon Jovi."

My mouth fell open. I stood there speechless, watching him walk down the hallway.

I watched as he swiped his badge outside the doorway and slipped inside the room near the end of the hall. *Where did he go?* Looking around, I was the only one in the hall. I followed behind him and peered through the small glass pane in the door. There was a security lock for a badge swipe on the doorknob. I tried to swipe my badge when a beep alarm and error message read, NO ACCESS.

My immediate thoughts were *a blue shirt, blue jeans, black boots, and sexy hair.*

He DOES look like Jon Bon Jovi!

It was Friday, and I was eating alone. I had not seen him since Tuesday morning, when he slipped into the computer room. Susannah took the day off to start her anniversary weekend with her husband. In the courtyard, on a beautiful sunny day, I was having lunch alone. When I noticed the main building's door open and, in my peripheral, I saw … *It's him, oh God. Stay calm.*

On his way to the breakroom, he walked right by me. The windows allowed him to see me, so I kept my eyes on my book, but

I had not read one word. He walked out of the breakroom a moment later and straight towards my table.

He sat across from me.

"You alone today?" he asked.

I smiled. "Yes, Susannah is off today, and Rita moved to the customer service department."

"Is that a good book? I heard a movie is coming out," he said.

"Yeah, I'm finishing the series before it does."

"Is your printer working better?"

"Yes, thanks for sending Paulie over to fix it."

He stood up and walked away. "Send me a message if you need anything else."

Quietly, I smiled to myself. *So, you do like me.*

While the Cat's Away

Susannah and I continued our walk on the track during break time. "Are you still dating that guy in the Air Force?" she asked.

I wished I hadn't lied or shared so much about my life with her.

"Danny? No. I broke up with him a while ago. He was always gone and didn't want a serious relationship with me. I don't want to confuse Freddy with a guy who comes in and out of my life. I'm looking for someone who can handle us both."

"Yeah, that's good. You both are a package deal," she added.

"I'm only asking because Freece sent me a chat message asking if you were dating anyone."

I stopped walking.

"Oh?!" My smile gave me away.

"Would you consider a date with him? He is a nice guy. I may have mentioned that you have a son, and he said, 'I don't care about that,'" she said.

I watched her, expecting a funny remark. She was serious.

"He's a good guy; I wouldn't mention him if I didn't think so. Besides, you deserve a good guy," she said.

I suddenly saw Susannah in a different light.

"Thanks, I'll think about it," I said with a huge grin, and butterflies filled me.

That weekend, Freddy and I stayed inside the apartment. He had a cold and wasn't feeling well. Mama and Liv came over while Liv went with me to get my grocery shopping done. It was nice to be alone with her. She shared her plans for a wedding and having children with Carter.

"I'm so happy for you, Liv. I like Carter. He's a great guy."

"I know, I can't believe it either. He is so good to me, and we get along so well. We love to spend time at home doing nothing but watching television and cooking. He loves to cook, and I love to watch television," she laughed.

"Well … I was going to…" I began when she interrupted.

"Mama and Rico like him, too. I'm excited about the day you find a boyfriend so we can go out together."

She will not stop talking.

"Well, there's one guy at work," I finally blurted. I gave a look in her direction to see her response.

"Oh really! Tell me more," she said, tugging at a shopping cart.

"His name is Freece Miles. He works in IT. He is charming, kind, and a little older than me, but I'm unsure how old." I stopped talking to help her untangle the carts. "I know little about him; we have only spoken a few times."

"Why not invite him out for lunch one day, not at work. I don't recommend spending time with a coworker at the workplace. If things don't work out, seeing him after the breakup is not good," she said.

"I agree; I thought about that too, but I don't see Freece at work anyway, so if we did date and break up, it would be easy to avoid him," I admitted.

Liv continued pushing the cart while I dropped various groceries into it. Not really thinking about all that I needed.

"Let me know if you ask him; I would love to meet him. Mama and I used to wonder what kind of guy would be good enough for Vivian," she said.

Returning to work felt good after a relaxing weekend. I didn't mind the morning drive; as time passed, dropping Freddy at daycare had become less painful for us both. Every day, he would stretch his arms and call out to me in tears as I walked away. The daycare staff told me he was better within minutes. I'd sit in the car having to compose myself and often wondered if it was a mistake to do everything on my own. I knew having a job was necessary, but still I hoped I could provide more for Freddy.

While at work, I suddenly snapped out of my daydream upon hearing that familiar bell sound: *brr-rink*. That sound made me stop what I was typing and look. *Who was messaging me?* The notification blinking …

Susannah was typing …

Slopez@billing: Good morning. I am not taking a morning break today. I'll see you at lunch.

Vperez@billing: No worries. Is everything okay?

Slopez@billing: I have a lot to catch up on and want to finish before lunch. See you then.

The morning was the same; I stayed at my desk during the break to enjoy a second cup of coffee and read. It was 10:10 a.m., and I heard the sound again. *Brr-rink.*

I opened the message.

Fmiles@it: How was your weekend?

Oh, boy! It was him. It was Freece. This was not about work; he was asking me a personal question—no harm in answering it.

Vperez@billing: Good, thanks. How was your weekend?

Fmiles@it: It was good; I was in the pool all weekend and watched a few movies. Grilled some steaks.

Vperez@billing: Yes, it was very relaxing for me, too. I stayed home watching TV and went boring grocery shopping—steaks and a pool sound good. I had leftovers and ham sandwiches.

Fmiles@it: I'll let you know the next time I grill steaks. You and your son should come swimming.

What was happening here? Was he asking me out? He just mentioned my son. The cursor is blinking, so he knew I was waiting to type...

Vperez@billing: Cool. That sounds like fun. Sure, let me know when.
Vperez@billing: Also, how did you know I have a son?

Fmiles@it: A little bird may have told me.

Vperez@billing: Was that "little bird" named Susannah?

Fmiles@it: I will let you know the next time I start the grill.

I sent Susannah a message.
Vperez@billing: I hope you can finish all that work during your break. I just got a message from Freece that a "little bird" was talking to him about me.

Slopez@billing: This little bird is always here to help. I'm glad the two of you are finally talking. Let me know if you need help with anything else.

During lunch, we laughed and joked about my morning talk with Freece.

"I know he bought a house and lives in St. Petersburg or Clearwater. But I didn't know he had a pool. So, do you think you'll go swimming with him?"

"I don't know. That is a lot for a first date, you know? Taking my one-year-old son to have steak."

We laughed.

"Not to mention wearing a bathing suit on a first date at his house. I may have to suggest a new idea for our meeting outside of work. And 'little bird,' do you mind not saying anything else to him? I want this to come from him and not feel you are pushing it," I said as I gave her the side eye.

"That's fine. I just wanted to give a little push, that's all. I'm done," she said, raising her hands.

The rest of the week, I saw Freece walking through the courtyard during lunch; he came over once and said hello to us, but no conversations about his house. I may have scared him away when he realized I had a son. On Friday, I finally felt ready to message him.

Vperez@billing: Hello. Happy Friday! Are you available for lunch this weekend? I want to take you out to one of my favorite places. Warning: It is not steak.

Fmiles@it: Sure. I'm available on Saturday or Sunday.

Vperez@billing: Tomorrow is good. Call or text, and I can tell you where to meet at 12:30 p.m.

I messaged my phone number, and there it was. A new friendship began based on a ham and cheese sandwich.

After work, I went by to pick up Freddy from Mama's and had dinner with them.

"Mama, would you be available tomorrow to watch Freddy?"

"Sure, I'll take him to the aquarium."

"That sounds good; I was thinking about going to lunch with a friend from work."

It felt good to finally be honest with mama, even if I wasn't telling her who.

"Yeah, tomorrow is good. I can pick Freddy up by nine o'clock in the morning. Have him dressed and ready," she said.

That was easy, and it would give me time to get myself ready.

After they left for the aquarium, I got dressed. I made it simple by wearing a tee shirt, shorts, and flip-flops. There was no way I was going to wear a bathing suit on our first date. I wanted Freece to see me in my casual daily look. Not the "business casual" he was used to.

He called me at noon.

"Hello there. How have you been?" Freece asked.

"I'm good. Are you hungry?"

"I am. Where would you like to meet?"

"Do you know Jersey Jo's Deli on St. Pete Beach?"

"I've seen it but never been there."

"Cool, let's meet there at 12:30. Then we can go to my other favorite place," I said.

"Sounds good. See you then."

I left the house with my beach bag filled with a blanket, towels, and wallet. When I arrived, it was 12:35. I saw the black truck parked as I drove into Jersey Jo's. I took a deep breath. *Here we go.*

I first noticed his legs! Wow! He looked so different, dressed in a white tee shirt with a bar logo on the back, black board shorts, and brown flip-flops. His hair was perfectly messy.

"Did you have any traffic?" he asked.

"Just a little coming over the bridge. Sorry, I'm late."

"No problem, I live 15 minutes from here. Did you come from Tampa?"

"Just north of Tampa, in Carroll Pines."

We ordered our sandwiches to go.

"I was thinking we could go eat on the beach?"

"That sounds good. I haven't been to the beach in years," he confessed.

"We can take my car. I'll drive."

We spread the blanket on the sand and enjoyed our sandwiches while talking and listening to the waves. The sun was warm, and the breeze helped to keep us cool. Engaged in conversation, we enjoyed the day chatting about everything and nothing in particular. I found comfort in his presence and his soothing tone. I repeatedly wiped my mouth each time he stared at me.

I hope I have nothing on my face.

Interstate Love

The day was perfect, and I knew this spot was peaceful. Mostly locals visited this beach, and few tourists knew about it. I wanted a place where we could talk and get to know each other without distractions. After we finished eating, we walked along the shore. Neither of us said which direction to go or what to do next. There were moments when Freece would stop talking and look at me. I wondered what he was thinking …

He stopped walking, and with a half a grin, he smiled at me.

"What? Do I have something on my nose?"

"Nothing. I was just thinking about a trip to Italy I took."

We both continued walking with quick glances back and forth at each other.

"Have you ever been?"

"Italy? I would love to go there. That's one of the top five places I want to see. When did you go?"

He shared how he and his friend, Colby, had been to France and Prague. He flew with the Tampa Hockey team to Prague and spent time with the players.

"You should go with us next time."

I'll pretend that I didn't hear that.

"My life is not as thrilling as yours. I had plans to go to college after graduation, but after having Freddy, I changed my plans."

"What were you going to college for? What major?" he asked.

"Um. I never thought about what I would go to college for. I figured I'd learn that in college." I laughed.

"Well, that is the great thing. You don't have to go at a certain age. Go when you're ready. Maybe having Freddy meant you weren't ready. When the time is right, you'll know what to do," he said.

This man was brilliant. He spoke without judgment.

"Did you go to college to study IT?" I asked.

"No, actually my degree is in finance and accounting," he admitted.

"Oh really? That's interesting."

He told the story of how he worked as an accountant after college and then moved to Florida, where he took a job at Credential Services in the finance department. He stumbled across his IT skills by accident and was noticed by the supervisor. Later, he went back to college, earned his certifications, and changed his job position.

"So you see, you don't have to know what you want to do in college. Because life can change."

We got to the end of the beach, where the wall of rocks turned from gray to black as the water splashed against them.

"So, why are you still single?" I asked.

"I'm single by choice. Not because I don't want a relationship, just that I have found no one that can live up to my standards and expectations." He stopped walking and turned around. "Usually, I'm a quiet person. I like to keep to myself. You seem to make me comfortable enough to talk."

I stopped walking. He turned toward me.

"What? Is that a problem?" he asked.

"No. I feel the same way. I'm just surprised that you said it."

We continued walking.

"Okay, I'll bite. What are your standards and expectations? Since this is our 'getting to know you date,' you go first," I said.

"There are a couple of things I look for in someone I'd consider being in a relationship with. No smoking, not a party girl, and I used to think I didn't want kids. But I've changed my mind on that one. And I have a few others, but I'll keep those to myself and see how this goes," he said with a smile.

With a raised eyebrow and a smile, I silently hoped he didn't notice.

"Hmm. Interesting! I have a few standards and expectations, too."

He smiled. We were back on the blanket and sitting beside each other, watching the sky, and listening to the water splash ahead of us. I kicked off my flip-flops and buried my toes in the sand.

"So, are you gonna tell me your expectations?" he asked.

"The no-smoking is good. I'll add that to my list. I agree, no partying. Having one or two drinks is good, but I've never been one for heavy drinking. And, of course, kids. I'll be honest: my son Freddy isn't your regular kid. He's better than most. So, it's a good thing you changed your expectations and allowed kids, or we would have to stop this date now and never see this beautiful sunset together."

Neither of us said anything more. We had shared enough for today. I walked away, knowing more than I expected, and everything was perfect.

It had been two weeks since Freece and I went on our first date. I finally took some time to visit with Mama and Rico. I was excited to share my story about meeting him. As I prepared the salad, I could sense that Mama had something she wanted to say.

"So, Olivia came by yesterday."

Here we go.

She stopped, waiting for me to ask. So, I did. "Oh yeah? What did Olivia have to say?"

I knew where this was going.

"Oh, not much. She may have mentioned that you met someone at work. Is that true?"

Geesh Liv. Can you not keep anything to yourself.

"Well, yeah, there is this one guy. We went on a lunch date to the beach. He lives in Saint Petersburg and has a home with a swimming pool. Originally, he's from New York, and goes back to visit his family once a year."

Rico was eating carrots as fast as I could cut them. He gave a thumbs up when I mentioned *he's from New York.*

"What's his name? Maybe I know him," Rico said, adding salad to his bowl.

I shook my head at Rico. "I doubt that. He's from Hudson, New

York."

"Yeah, that's up-state. I don't know him."

"Anyway. He's a huge Tampa Bay Lightning fan and has season tickets to the New York Yankees' spring training in Tampa."

"I love this guy," Rico was quick to speak, as he grabbed cucumbers while I cut them.

I continued, "He plays hockey once a week. He and his friend, Colby, travelled to Italy and France and intend to visit London soon. We've talked for hours over the phone. I find him so interesting. When I asked if he had ever been married, he said, 'No, I'm still waiting for the right one to come along.'" I could barely stop rambling.

Rico interrupted. "He sounds good enough for me to date him. I want to go with him to see the Yankees and the Lightning play."

"It seems you had a nice first date, and you like him," Mama said.

"I do. But it is still early. We have only been talking over chat messages and phone calls. Going to the beach that once was our first date, and I want to take it slowly and not rush my feelings before I include Freddy. It's too soon to include Freddy right now."

"Si, mi amor. That is good advice. Be careful with Freddy's feelings, too."

"I am. That's why I am in control of when we talk and don't talk. I told Freece I am not being hurtful or mean, but I must go at a pace I can control because I have a son. He said he would do the same if he had a daughter."

"Wait. Don't you work together?" Rico asked.

"We work at the same location but rarely see each other. We both agreed to keep our relationship discreet at work, to avoid gossip or conflicts of interest. He keeps it very professional. I like that about him; it prevents me from being pressured at work."

"I'm liking this Freece even more now. I cannot wait to meet him," Mama said.

"Me, too. Tell Freece I like hockey," Rico said.

On Monday morning I left early to drop Freddy at daycare and the black truck was already there. I went inside and standing near my cubicle was Freece.

"Did you get my message?"

"No. What did it say?" I tried to hold back my smile.

"You'll have to listen to it when you get home today. I gotta go."

He rushed away. He would do that throughout the day. Stop by and peek over my cubicle while walking through our department. I started hearing this rustling sound against the outside of my cubicle. I'd stand up to see who or what it was, and then I'd see him leaving the department. I'd sit down and try to hold my laughter. *He's flirting with me! So much for keeping it professional.*

After a hectic day of picking up Freddy and rushing home through traffic, I completely forgot about the voicemail. My hands were full as I walked inside. Dropping my lunch bag and purse, I hit the button on the machine and remembered as soon as I heard his voice.

"Good morning! I figured you were on your way to work now, so I wanted to leave this for you. I hope you had a nice day. That's all."

On Tuesday, there was another voicemail. "Happy Tuesday! By the time you get this, there will be three more days to go until the weekend."

Each day, he would stop by my desk and ask me, "Did you get my message?"

"Happy Wednesday. I'll be working at the other building for the rest of this week, in case you miss seeing me."

Each day, his message would mean so much more.

In the past, I rarely received a phone call from Danny unless he was leaving a voicemail with a time and a room number. But now, with Freece, I found myself checking my answering machine as soon as I got home. I was eager just to hear his voice. He was so sweet.

I called Carter. "I have a question for you."

"Okay. Shoot!"

"Have you ever listened to voice messages from another phone?"

"Oh sure. You just have to create a PIN and when you call your house number, you'll enter the PIN and it will allow you to listen to your messages."

"Brilliant! Thanks, Carter."

"Sure, no problem, kid. I'll see ya."

After a few tries, I figured it out. The next day at work, I remembered to call my voicemail and there he was. Just eight minutes ago, he had left the message.

"Happy Thursday! I've been installing computers in the new administrative building. I'll be back next week. Or maybe sooner."

On Friday morning, I was too busy to check my voicemail. I was deep into work when I heard a rustle against my cubicle. I stood up and he was pushing a cart of monitors down the hall. When he saw me stand up, he gave me a wave. And a beautiful smile.

I took a minute and called my voicemail. I called and listened to it twice.

"Happy Friday! I wanted to know if you would like to go see the Lightning play this weekend, on Saturday night? I would have given you more notice, so you'd have time to get a sitter for Freddy, but I just got the extra ticket confirmed. I'll call you tonight after work. After you get this message."

I hung up and shuffled some paperwork around, feeling giddy and playful. I called Mama.

"Hey Mama. I'm at work, so I can't talk for long. I just wanted to see if you could watch Freddy tomorrow night?"

"Ay, si. You got a hot date con Freez?"

Hoping the chatter of printers and computers humming would block out my voice, I whispered, "Well, actually, yes. He asked me to go with him to the hockey game Saturday night."

"Ay mi amor. That sounds like a fun time for you. I can pick up Freddy in the morning and he can stay over-the-night until Sunday with us?"

"Are you sure, Mom?"

"Of course, I'm sure. I'll call you in the morning."

Now I just needed to come up with a plan as clever as his daily voicemails. Then I realized he doesn't know that I know he asked me to go to the game. I called his phone, and I left a voicemail.

"HAPPY FRIDAY! I would love to go to the Lightning game with you! And my mom has volunteered to keep Freddy all day Saturday until Sunday! Would you like to go to lunch on Saturday and then we can go to the game that night? Call me once you get this message. I'll be in my cubicle working."

Feeling a little scattered, I put on my headphones and began typing. With a little pep in my step, I was smiling and feeling good.

Imagine how he will feel when he gets home and hears that message.

Immediately after work, I rushed home and ordered a pizza for dinner. I listened to the voice message again.

And I waited.

At 7:08, the phone rang! I let it ring three times before I picked it up. I didn't want him to know that I had been sitting with the phone in my lap since I got home. Well, except for the few minutes to open the door for the pizza delivery and contemplating whether or not Freddy needed a bath before he fell asleep. There was no way I could leave the phone unattended for that long. Besides, Mama would give him a bath tomorrow.

"Hello!" I lowered my voice, hoping to sound sexy, as I wiped pizza sauce off my face and my shirt.

"Hello there. How are you?" he asked.

"I'm good, so ..."

"So, I got your voicemail!" he laughed.

"You did? Huh!"

"I'd love to have lunch tomorrow."

I could hear the smile in his voice.

"And I'd love to go to the Lightning game with you tomorrow night," I played along.

"And I'd love to have breakfast with you on Sunday morning?!"

Silence!

I swallowed hard on a piece of pepperoni and coughed. I wasn't ready for that one.

I prefer when he leaves a voicemail instead. It gives me time to react.

This was live!

"You okay? I was just going to tell you we could *meet* at the Breakfast Spot on Sunday morning, or I can make breakfast for you here at my house. Don't decide now. We can talk at the game."
And breathe.

SUMMER'S LAST HOO-RAH!

Freddy was turning two that summer, and I'd been reflecting a lot. I tried to call Danny when I heard the message he left on my phone.

"Let's meet tonight at the beach at six o'clock, room 112."

I tried to call him back, but he didn't answer. It was a good thing, for once. *I can't believe I said that.*

It's incredible what you can see about yourself when you step away and look at things from a different perspective. I saw Danny differently now after spending time with Freece.

We talked on the phone every night. He shared stories about his parents and cousins up north. He even invited me to New York and a trip to Italy. I dismissed the idea, but hoped we would talk about it again.

My phone rang; excitedly I answered, "Hello?"

"Hey darlin', how ya doin'? Can you talk?"

It was Danny.

"Did you get my message about tonight?" he asked.

"Yes, I did. I would like to get together. Let me check with my mom to see if she can watch Freddy. I'll call you back."

I decided I had to let Danny go, or even better, cut off contact with him altogether. He only called me for the wrong reasons—shame on me.

I felt guilty for leaving Freddy with Mama on those nights that I would meet Danny. It gave us time to reminisce. We eventually stopped discussing us as a couple. Initially, I was fine with it. But at this point, I felt I should let him go.

I've asked myself a million times why I stayed with him. My only answer was that we were familiar with one another. We laughed and had sex. A lot of sex! There was one thing we had in common. We fulfilled each other's needs. We were so open with one another about sex. But … There was always a but. But we had nothing else in common.

He seemed bored if I mentioned anything about my mom and sister. I didn't care to hear about his work or the issues he was having with his brother. He never discussed his parents back in Spring Mountain. He still wasn't interested in having children. I thought maybe I stayed with him, hoping one day he would change. He wouldn't.

Once, I tried to tell him about the new guy I met to see if he would get jealous, and he just changed the subject by tickling me and kissing me.

"Does the new guy do this to you, though?"

We wrestled and had more sex. I realized this was our pattern that I no longer wanted to continue.

I pulled into the parking lot and paid the fee. Before I got out of the car, I noticed I had a missed text.

Freece: What are you and Freddy doing tonight? How about dinner and some ice cream?

Me: That sounds good, but I have plans with my mom tonight. Raincheck?

Freece: Sure. We'll talk soon. Have a good night. Tell Freddy I said hello.

Fridays after five o'clock was always busy at the Surfside Inn. The Tiki bar was alive with happy hour until seven. I saw Danny sitting at the bar, munching on some chips and salsa. He did not expect me until 7:00. Instead, unlike my usual routine, I didn't go straight to the room to await him. I walked over to the bar and sat at the far end. I saw he was facing away from me, looking at the beach. He was wearing his bathing suit, no shirt, and the same baseball cap he'd always worn. His tan muscles gleamed with sweat, or he had been in the pool. Two hours early, I realized he must do this before I arrived. I loved watching him look out at the beach.

The bartender asked, "What can I get you?"

I wanted a real drink to get me through this next hour, but I knew his next question would be, "Can I see your ID?" So, I played it safe and ordered my usual.

"I'll have a Coke on the rocks, straight up, with a straw."

The bartender gave me a curious look and a smile. "No one's ever ordered a Coke like that," he said.

My eyes looked up and noticed Danny was standing. I watched him grab his beer.

"I heard you from over there and knew only one person orders their coke that way."

He smiled and lifted his eyebrows. Those eyebrows could dance if he let them. He was beautiful, and I was about to let him go, breaking my heart. He leaned in and kissed me twice.

"You're early."

"You're welcome. I came straight from work, and Mama was picking up Freddy from daycare for me. We could walk the beach a little before."

His eyebrows danced again. "Before what?" he smirked.

I left cash on the bar and took my Coke with me.

"Shut up. Let's walk and enjoy this weather."

The beach was warm. The sand was cool and wet. I liked to walk along the waterline and let the splash cool my legs. We never held hands. I never noticed that before. Today, I saw everything. This might be our first time walking on the beach during the daytime. Usually, we would walk along the beach afterward, but it would always be during the night. Often, after midnight, we would get a burst of energy and go to Tiki Hut for snacks and a walk by the water. We never held hands then, either.

I felt something—anger and aggravation with Danny. It was time to tell him and explain how this no longer worked for me. I could turn this around and see if I could change his mind on marriage and children. One last plea to see if he may want that with me. Then he could tell me, *yes, of course, I would rather be together than lose you. Let's plan a marriage with children and stay together* or I could tell him I've met someone new and let him go.

"What do you think about me getting an apartment in Tampa near the water? It will cost more, but I'll check out various places to see which I can afford," he said. And he never said *we* could check out places near the water.

Now was good.

"Danny, we need to talk. I am happy for you and your job situation. I'm sure you will find a great place along the water. You could check out Harbour Island or Davis Island areas; both are nice. But I have to break up with you now, right now. I have loved you and made love to you for two years, but this is no longer what I want. You are beautiful inside and out, but I want more. I have been lying to you," I said.

He stopped walking and turned toward me. I had waited until we were further down the beach, and no one else was around to hear. But now I realized we were far from the parking lot, which could get uncomfortable.

"Seriously, you're breaking up with me. We aren't even a couple," he said.

Ouch! That hurts.

"I know. What I mean is that I must break off what we have been doing. Meeting at the hotel secretly, having sex and then never seeing each other until the next time you decide to send me a message. I want more."

There I said it.

"I am at a point in my life where having a son makes a difference. You and I never wanting the same things is fine for you. I can respect that and wish you the best. But I respect myself more. I no longer want to show up like a puppy waiting for my treat. I want to be with someone who wants to be with me. Kids or no kids, marriage or not."

I stopped talking. I had said too much. But I'd said it. I'd had those thoughts for a while and was glad I'd finally shared them. Danny was silent.

"Aren't you going to say something?" I asked.

"Yes, of course…. I am going to miss you. I care about you, too. But I would do the same thing if I had a son," he said.

His words hit me hard. *If I had a son.*

That made me go silent.

We turned around and walked back. I counted the steps left until we returned to Tiki Hut. I knew that distance was all I had left; it would be the perfect time to tell him. He squeezed my hand firmly, and I realized we were holding hands.

We were still walking.

"I wish things were different, but you should do what is best for you and your son. I have always told you I'm not the 'settle down' type, and I can't make promises I won't keep," he said.

We stopped walking only halfway to the parking lot.

He leaned over and picked me up. I wrapped my legs around him and my arms around his shoulders and neck. We kissed. People were everywhere now.

We didn't care. We pulled away from each other's lips and looked into each other's eyes. I saw the sadness in him, and I realized he cared. We walked, and he grabbed my hand again.

I guided us toward the car, and he playfully pulled my hand toward the hotel.

"You sure?" He joked.

But I wouldn't. I pulled our hands back towards me, guiding us toward my car.

"I truly will miss you—your smile. You have the best smile."

And that made me smile more. We hugged again, and this time, I wept.

"I'll miss you, too. I loved you," I said, wiping my eyes.

"I loved you, too."

As I got in the car, I put on my seatbelt and lowered the radio's volume. He stood there while I lowered the window for him to lean in.

"I'll never forget you. Maybe one day we can find each other again." I smiled.

The drive home was long. I had been over that bridge many times; the Bay of Tampa was quiet today. No boats or jet skis were on the silver glass of the water below.

The traffic was low, and my car was the only one on the bridge. A few people were walking along the Courtney Campbell

Trail. I had always wanted to walk along the trail and had yet to take the time to do that.

I have time now.

Part Nine

A Bride

FALL

There was a shift in the weather and a slight temperature change. It was the humidity that was missing. Seventy-one degrees in the winter was pleasant, but I needed a sweater when the temperature dropped to the sixties.

"All my years living in New York, I would never wear a sweater until the temperature hit the 50s. Living in Florida, I get cold at 65," Freece said.

"Do you still consider yourself a New Yorker?" I asked.

"Hey, once a New Yorker, always a New Yorker! But the warm weather is something I enjoy. I'm done with snow."

I learned early on that he said precisely what he was thinking. He never held back, and I admired that. So, when he told me, "I love you so much," I believed him.

Freece and I enjoyed working together in the kitchen. I chopped the vegetables while he cooked over the stove.

"So, I wanted to ask you about your plans for Thanksgiving. My mom has invited us to her and Rico's house. My sister and her husband will be there, too."

He smiled. "Really? I would like that. I usually make a turkey and all the fixings for myself. It would be nice to be with you and Freddy. And your family, too. Can I still bring something?"

"Yes, of course. My mom would love that. What can you make?"

"Anything. I'll bring a pie and green bean casserole," Freece replied.

I couldn't help but laugh.

"What's so funny? I like to cook and bake," he said.

"No, nothing is funny about that. It's great. I love that about you," I said.

He stopped and turned toward me. "You love me?"

"Uh! I love THAT about you," I stammered.

"Oh! So you don't love me, just my cooking? Okay, because I was about to say that *I love you!*"

I took a breath and smiled. "Yes, I love you! There, I said it!"

He put down the spatula, turned toward me, and picked me up.

"Thank God you said it first. I've been waiting to say those words!"

"You said it first. I just said I loved your cooking."

We embraced, and he swung me around, laughing and kissing my neck.

I have always loved fall. The change in vibe of the people seems sweeter and kinder. It's the joyful sounds of Christmas music whispering above as we strolled through the mall. And then there's the traffic. Freece hated traffic.

"Where are all these people during the rest of the year? Why do they wait until tonight to come out? This town needs public transportation. I mean, what the hell?" Freece snapped.

And Freddy repeated, "What the hell?"

"Babe, you gotta watch your mouth," I said, holding back a laugh.

"I'm sorry, but …," he said.

And I shook my head. "No. No buts."

And Freddy, on repeat, "No. But."

"We need to choose better words to use around him. Look at the spectacular weather we are having. Isn't the traffic horrendous tonight? The stars are in a beautiful array in the sky," I said.

And we awaited Freddy's echo. I glanced back and noticed him in a trance, fixated on the movie that was playing on the screen.

"I've been looking at a new place for dinner next week. I'd like to take you and Freddy to. Are you good with that?" he asked.

"Sure, just let me know when."

He always planned and searched for new places to check out. I loved that he was a planner because I was not. It was nice to arrive at Mama and Rico's place for dinner after a day at the mall. Sundays had become the night we had family dinners with them. Liv and Carter made it most of the time. I had seen my mom more these past five months than I had all year.

Freece loved family time, which made me curious why he had moved so far away from his family in New York. But I was happy that he did.

THE ROUND HOTEL

There was an unexplainable and indescribable feeling that existed. I felt as though I had known Freece forever. It was *comfortable.* We blended well together, making our transition to how we spent our nights together at my apartment and some nights at his house. Freddy moved back and forth seamlessly.

We still considered it as "Freece's house" and "our apartment". But Freddy walked into each one with his toys and a bedroom at both. His own space.

"I never want you to feel that you and Freddy can't be here. And when you are, I want him to be comfortable."

He knew that as long as Freddy was good, I was good. And it was in those moments that made me love him more.

We drove together Friday after work to pick up Freddy from daycare. Saturday morning, the three of us got up early and headed to St. Petersburg Beach. Freece preferred St. Pete Beach over Clearwater because he hated Clearwater's traffic. It had become such a popular beach with the tourists.

We planned to stay one night at the hotel on the beach and relax. We had never taken a staycation together. One nice thing about Florida was being able to go to the beach in December. Hotel prices had dropped, and the beaches were deserted. Despite swapping a bathing suit for a sweater, it remained a lovely day and night. Along the Gulf, we walked, played, and enjoyed reading stories on a hammock. They had fire pits and chairs around to sit and cook s'mores. Freece and I enjoyed a bottle of wine and watched Freddy play in the sand.

There were parts of St. Pete Beach that had been there for years. There was one hotel that I had always known and loved each time we drove to the beach. The Reef Resort distinguished itself from the rest, with its cylindrical shape and stunning white seashell paint. The windows were lined with sea green tiles that gave a shimmer to draw you closer. From a distance, the building looked white and green striped. I always loved driving towards the beach and seeing this hotel. It was a beautiful building that had been around since the 1970s. On the top floor, there was a restaurant called *360*. Like the name, it slowly gave a complete rotation, with amazing views of the water and beaches in all directions.

Freece picked up Freddy and pointed to the top of the round hotel.

"Can you see the top of the building there? See those windows?" he asked.

Freddy replied, "Yeah."

"Well, that's where we're eating dinner tonight."

And they both looked over at me with smiles. We took the elevator up and it opened right into the restaurant. The rotation was so slow that you could barely notice the movement.

"I was worried I would feel nauseous looking out, but it's beautiful," I whispered to Freece.

"We have reservations under Freece Miles for a party of three," he announced to the host.

"Yes, Mr. Miles, we have your table ready for you," the host replied, with menus in hand.

She guided us to a table by the window, adorned with elegant white and gold plates, and lit candles to create a warm ambiance. It was early, and the few people there were whispering to one another. Plates and glasses were clinking.

"This place is too romantic to have Freddy with us," I whispered.

"No. Not at all. I want him to be with us for all these fun vacations."

We had a beautiful dinner, and just sitting there as we slowly spun around kept Freddy's eyes looking out the window. He could see down to the beach. Tiki lamps and fire pits were lit, and people walked and danced down the coast. It was a beautiful night—a perfect dinner as the sun settled on the water.

After finishing a bottle of Cabernet and watching Freddy eat some ice cream, Freece excused himself to the men's room. I sat and watched the view. This was all new for Freddy and me. I could see myself having this always.

"Freddy, what do you think of all this?" Freece said as he approached the table.

He was still standing and looking out the window.

"Are you ready to go? He's not done with his ice cream, and I still have half a glass," I said, not wanting to leave.

He leaned down to tie his shoe.

"No. I have one more thing to do," he said in a mumble.

He got down on one knee beside me and presented a black velvet box. He was frozen, with his eyes locked onto mine. I could tell that he was nervous, and I looked at him in surprise. His eyes welled up in tears, his words were soft. "Vivian Perez, will you marry me and allow me to be with you and Freddy for the rest of my life?"

Freddy heard his name and glanced at Freece and then at me. My eyes must have shown shock and surprise. I didn't realize what was happening initially, and then it came at me in a rush.

He's proposing.

He looked at me with those big blue eyes still kneeling there, waiting.

"Yes. Yes. I will marry you!"

I reached over to hug Freece, and he hugged us both. The crowd cheered when we released our embrace. The staff had champagne for everyone—compliments of The Reef Resort. Freece placed the ring on my finger. It was beautiful.

"Once we are married, I want Freddy to have my last name too," he said.

We left with congratulations from everyone in the room. While in the elevator, Freddy held my finger with a newly engaged shiny ring. We joked about the size and sparkle.

"If ships were lost at sea, your ring could guide them back to land," Freece said.

In our room, we settled Freddy for the night. I was glad that we had the suite. The bedroom had sliding glass doors leading to the balcony overlooking the gulf. We sat outside, holding each other in silence. We listened to the sounds of the swoosh and sway; the water was talking to us, and we were there to listen. I marked today as the perfect day.

"No other day can be better than this," I said.

And Freece softly whispered, "Until the day of our wedding."

New York's Not My Home

We took a week's vacation to New York. It had been almost four years since Freece had been home. The last time he had gone back to Hudson was for his cousin's wedding.

Today, we flew to Hudson because he wanted to show us where he was from. Freddy found enjoyment in looking out the window and seeing the clouds below us. After we were settled and in flight, he chose a movie. I leaned towards Freece, not realizing the pain that would come from my next question. "What made you move away from New York?"

Freece began telling me the story of his life in Hudson.

"I have never shared the full story of why I moved away from Hudson with anyone. But I want you to know everything about me," he said. "You know, it was just my mom and me growing up, and I used to go back and forth visiting my dad over the summers. My dad moved to Vermont when I was fourteen for a new job position. He would come to visit each winter until the year I turned nineteen. He could no longer drive, so I began the drive to see him. A few months prior, he'd received a cancer diagnosis and had to stop working. He had hoped the treatment would remove it all, but it was in his blood. For the first time, my mom said she would travel with me. She felt this would be my last time seeing Dad."

"Would you like a drink?" the flight attendant interrupted.

Freece and I had a glass of wine. Freddy pulled his headphones off and looked over at me.

"Would you like some juice?" I asked.

Excitedly, he pulled down the tray and placed his drink and

snack on top. Occasionally, he would peek out the window and glance at the clouds hoping to see more.

Freece had bought him a kid's camera the week before. He had such a fun time clicking every shot. I knew he had taken most photos as blurred snaps along his walk, and I would have to delete them. But with the others that turned out clear, we planned to create a photo album for him to keep as a reminder of his first family vacation.

After he cleaned up snack time, he reclined his seat and continued his movie. Freece went on with his story.

"Because I was traveling with my mom, we had booked a hotel room for her near Dad's house. He offered us the guest room, but she was uncomfortable with that. Usually, it was a three-and-half-hour drive, but Mom and I stopped for lunch, and the snow was falling heavily. It ended up being nearly five hours when we arrived at Dad's place. As soon as he opened the door, I saw he was not well. He was fragile, thin, and his face and hands were yellow. I sensed this would be my last time with him."

Freece stopped to wipe his tears. He was feeling the pain again.

"Are you okay?" I asked.

This must be why he had never told me his story. Freece stopped talking, and I held him. I was never good at comforting someone other than Freddy. But at this moment, with Freece, I knew we were sharing something that would only bring us closer.

It was here that Freddy needed to use the restroom. I had hoped we would not have to do that on an airplane. I had never liked public restrooms, but we had little choice at 35-thousand feet. This gave Freece a moment to get himself together. When we returned to our seats, I noticed he'd ordered two more glasses of wine. We settled again and quietly gave cheers, "To New York and a New Year. Cheers!"

"You don't have to tell the rest of your story," I said.

"I do. I want you to know everything," he continued. "That evening, we spent time with Dad. He was happy to have us both there. He told Mom he was glad she came along and hoped she had forgiven him for divorcing her. Through the years, he had thought about telling her that and now he could. You could see his guilt ease, which allowed him to have closure. And Mom needed that, too. It was a lovely night, watching *Jeopardy* and *Wheel of Fortune* together while we shared our dinner.

"I ended up staying four nights with Dad. Mom stayed at the hotel one day so I could spend it alone with him. He was too weak to get out and go anywhere, and the weather was too much for him to walk in. On our last day with Dad, we drove over and had breakfast with him. I had prepared myself for when I would say goodbye to him. I used the words, 'talk to you soon,' instead. I knew I would call him later that evening, once we were home, so I was not making this a goodbye." He began to tear up again. "I want to tell you before we land, but I'm not sure I can."

"Do you want to wait until we check in at the hotel, and then you can finish tonight?" I asked.

"No. I don't want each day on our vacation to be me crying, and still, I want you to understand everything that happened." He pressed on. "Mom and I left Dad's place, and I was a mess. Like I am right now. So, Mom said that she would drive home. At first, I didn't think she would be okay driving in the snow, but she insisted she had lived in New York all her life, and I needed to trust her. But neither of us knew the storm was already heading in our direction."

I stopped him and asked, "Wait. Is this the accident you told me that your mom was in?"

And with tears flowing down his face, he just nodded his head. "Yes." He cried.

Freece had told me that both his parents had passed away. His father died of cancer, and his mother died in a terrible car accident. It was our two-month dating anniversary, and we were sharing stories of our parents. I told him briefly about my dad and his controlling ways. I had not mentioned the abuse until after we were engaged. But, when he shared that his parents had passed away, he didn't tell me he was in the car with her on the night of the accident.

"We had just left Dad's house and gotten onto the highway when the snow fell heavily on the roads. It was coming down thick and fast. Mom pulled over onto the shoulder of the highway. She was having trouble seeing through the thick snow. We pulled off to the side and planned to switch places. It was just as I was walking in the snow, moving in front of our car, when I heard the screeching sounds from behind." He wiped his tears.

"And that is when the accident happened. It was a pileup of cars, one after another. Cars were slowing down and being pushed by the next. The snow was so thick and fog had rolled in, making it difficult to see the street in front of them. One after another, they rammed into the next, pushing each car onto the shoulder of the road. Those on the shoulder were pushed into the buildup of the others. It became a domino effect, and we had no chance to react as a semi-truck plowed into our vehicle, and before I could move out of the way, I was thrown.

I found myself stranded, and without my phone. I could see the headlights through a misty fog of snow. It was so thick and heavy. The sound of the cars screeching and banging into one another. I'm not sure why or how I knew to do what I did, but I began moving my arms and leg, like making a snow angel, to help clear the snow from under me. When I tried to stand, a sharp pain in my back and leg made it difficult. It was not until later that I realized I had broken my leg. Even though I screamed out for Mom, she didn't respond. The constant thought she was searching for me, hoping to hear my voice, I would scream out, 'I love you, Mom. I'm okay.'

It was later that I found out that she had died. The storm was reported as being a white-out."

He cleared his throat and wiped his eyes and nose. I was leaning forward in my seat and holding my breath with a hand to my mouth. Freddy looked over at us both and pulled his headphones off.

"What's wrong Mommy?"

"It's okay, buddy. I was telling Mom a sad story. We have twenty more minutes before we land. You excited?" Freece asked, wiping his eyes, and sniffling away the tears.

I sat back in my seat, stunned. I didn't know what to say.

Freece ended the story. "It took almost three hours for the fire trucks to get there since we were near the beginning of the crash. Two days later, my friend Colby drove up to get me. They had cleared and plowed the roads. I planned for Mom's body to be brought back to Hudson. A week later, Dad passed away at the Hospice. I wasn't there."

We landed!

"I need to step into the restroom and wash my face. Let's go buddy, we have a long drive still," Freece said as he took Freddy's hand.

Once we collected our baggage and made our way to the car rental, we then drove that same highway to Hudson.

"Are you going to be okay driving?" I asked.

"Yes, I'm fine. I have been here since the accident and it gets easier."

After our two-and-a-half-hour drive, we arrived at his cousin's home and spent the week enjoying our family time. Freddy had so much fun with his new cousins. He played in the snow and drank hot cocoa by the fireplace. Freece took us to "the hill", where we slid down on sleds. We walked around the shops on Warren Street. We stopped to have dinner and drinks at a few spots where live music was played. One song had me singing along with the sounds of a guitar slowly strumming: *New York's Not My Home*.

With a playful hip check, I walked hand in hand with Freece as the sun went down and Freddy raced ahead.

It was easy to see why he loved it there, but still I understood why he left and never moved back.

I Do, Too

Springtime in Florida was when the roses bloomed, and the azaleas were full. The crepe myrtles lined the drive of the park.

"The car will be here soon. Are you ready?" Liv asked.

"Freddy. Where is Freddy?"

"Mama is getting him."

"Let's get in the car now. I'm ready and have everything I need."

Mama walked in with Freddy. "The boys just left in the first car. It's safe for you to come out now."

Freddy, Mama, Liv, Rico, and I rode in the second car. We arrived at the park ten minutes later.

"I don't want him to see us until we reach the aisle," I said.

"Carter is making sure that Freece is turned around until you and Freddy get to the aisle," Rico said.

Just weeks before, we had both sat for hours listening to music; neither of us could choose the right song for me to walk the aisle to.

"Would you let me pick the song?" Freece asked, mostly because he saw I was struggling with all the decisions.

I was annoyed with the process of flowers, restaurants, a dress, shoes, makeup, hair, and getting Freddy ready, too. Having to pick music was more than I had patience for. I gratefully said, "Sure. I don't care," to whatever Freece chose.

I leaned down and reminded Freddy, "Walk, just like we practiced, down the aisle and stand beside Freece. You don't need to run. Be sure to walk so I can follow you."

I gave a nod to Carter. He tapped Freece on the shoulder to turn around.

Colby, pushed play, and the song that Freece had chosen began. *You Are the Reason,* by Calum Scott.

Mama and Rico walked first.

Liv walked next, wearing a soft green chiffon dress.

Freddy followed behind her.

Freece and Freddy stood sweetly together, waiting for me to meet them. Both were wearing light tan linen pants and matching white button-up shirts.

I walked the brick pathway alone, with a few friends and family watching.

I stood for a moment at the end of the walk, with the soft breeze against my ivory chiffon dress and a light veil down my long dark hair of soft waves. There in a white gazebo at a park by the bay, we stood together as the water gently lapped in the distance nearby. We shared our vows and promises to each other and to Freddy.

As the sun lowered itself from behind the clouds, the orange light shone down on us all.

"Do you, Vivian Perez, take Freece Miles to be your husband today, tomorrow, and forever?" the minister asked.

"I do."

And Freddy, staring at us both, said, "I do, too."

Everyone laughed. But Freddy was serious.

Somewhere Over the Rainbow

After the ceremony, we drove to the beach in Saint Petersburg and had a beautiful sunset dinner at the White Shell Restaurant. A spot that Freece and I had always talked of going to but knew the price was too high for our taste. Once we shared our wish list for our wedding dinner with Mama and Rico, it was a beautiful gift from them.

We knew we wanted to be in St. Pete; it was where we had our first date and being near the beach had always given us both comfort.

Freece had made reservations for us to stay at the hotel next door. By the time we said goodbye to everyone, it was after midnight. Freddy was asleep, still wearing his tan linen pants and now wrinkled shirt. I kissed him goodbye.

"Mommy and Daddy will be back soon," I leaned down and whispered.

"Where are you going?" he asked, his eyes still closed.

"Daddy and I are going to Hawaii, and you get to stay with Abuela and Abuelo Rico. We will be back soon," I said, kissing his forehead.

He fell back to sleep.

～

I should have planned better. By the time we went to sleep, it was nearly 2 am, and we were to be at the airport for a 7 am flight.

There we were, newly married and Freece with camera in hand. *Click!* It was the sound of his camera.

"You better get used to it. I plan to take over one thousand pictures this week."

"What are you taking pictures of?"

"You," he said.

"What? No. I don't think we should have any pictures of me at this hour, especially after only having four hours of sleep." I pushed away the camera. *Click, click, click* was a shot of my face and hand. He continued to take more.

"It's fine. Besides, who's going to see them but you and me, and you'll be glad we have them once we put them into an album."

After a delay in Phoenix, Arizona, we finally arrived at the Kahului airport. I felt fancy when I saw our limo driver holding a sign that read: Mr. and Mrs. Miles, Aloha! With beautiful leis for the two of us, we donned the beads and florals of the state.

I stared at Freece.

"What?" He turned and smiled.

"Nothing. Can't I stare at my husband? I just noticed that you have something on you." I pointed at him.

He turned around, trying to see it.

I grabbed his hand and said, "Oh, here it is! A big fat wedding band!" I laughed and pulled him close to me. "Can you believe we're married?"

"Yup! I always knew we would be." He leaned down and kissed me.

He was always the quiet loving guy. Not one for public displays of affection, but huge with sincere and tender touches. Of all the things I loved about him, it was that. Those moments were how I knew *he loved me*. The unspoken truths.

And that sexy wink he likes to give. He melts me.

Our driver took us to the hotel in Lahaina Shores. We were on the island of Maui, Hawaii. The weather was warm, like home. A constant breeze from the ocean beside us and a sweet scent of coconut and jasmine seemed to always be in the air.

We entered through a doorway, but still we remained outside. Countless wooden pillars filled the garden lobby. The courtyard was filled with beautifully carved beams shaped like Monstera leaves and lush tropical flowers gave a direct pathway to a view of the ocean.

The familiar ukelele sounds of Israel Kamakawi-wo'ole, *Somewhere Over the Rainbow,* softly played, with glasses of champagne awaiting us. It was a peaceful and cozy resort with only four floors. Just what we were hoping for - a week of relaxation. Our room had a balcony with a view of the Pacific, which not every room had. Each morning, we relished the view while indulging in coffee and room service breakfast. We spotted another island in the distance, and the dolphins came leaping out to greet us.

After a long day of traveling and barely any sleep, we held onto each other. We stayed until dark with the patio doors open and the breeze and sounds of the Pacific waves slamming in the distance. There we both laid, savoring the stillness of this time. Holding to each other, relaxing in this intimacy with touches and kisses. No words were spoken. Just the beauty of all that we had been through to get to this moment.

A short walk down Front Street led us to the quiet shops and restaurants where other honeymooners and locals browsed. It was hard to believe that we were still in the United States because so much about Hawaii made it feel as though we'd gone to another country. The locals had a calm and tranquil demeanor about them. There was no hustle or congestion of vehicles on the road. The locals rode bicycles or walked, and the streets were quiet and still.

Seeing this beautiful land and how much they loved and cared for it made me realize how different home was from here. Seeing the land through their eyes was pure beauty! It wasn't until night came and we were walking back to the hotel from dinner that I realized Lahaina didn't have streetlights, only small lamp posts. It was a radiant glow that came from the sky and illuminated our path with countless bulbs.

"Look at all those lights in the sky?"

"Stars!" Freece replied.

"Those are stars? They're so bright!"

"Well, those same stars are in the sky at home, too. You'll never see them because we have so much light pollution that our sky is never truly dark," Freece explained.

"I remember when I was younger, and we would have campfires at the back of Shannon's property. We could see the stars. I had forgotten that they were there."

We spent the next few days acting like tourists but felt like locals. You couldn't walk past the Oldest Banyan Tree without being pulled under. It was amazing. Sitting under its shade of enormous arms held out as though they were holding up the sky. There were some sitting and eating their lunch while children were dancing, and artists prepared their canvases. None were near us, yet all of us were under the same tree's arms. The enormity of it all was beautiful.

Over the few days, we took a driving tour along the Hana Highway. We stopped at the Dole Pineapple Museum, the shops, and a local vineyard. We ordered and shipped some bottles of what came to be our favorite wine.

"We should bring some of this banana nut bread back to the hotel," Freece suggested.

As he stood to pay for the bread and the wine, I heard the salesclerk say, "Congratulations!"

"For what?" Freece asked, thinking that he'd won a prize.

"Didn't you just get married?" she asked.

Grinning, he answered, "I did. But how did you know that?"

"Your ring is still shiny and new."

We laughed. As we walked away, I heard her say to the others in line, "We see new shiny rings all the time. Maui is the number one island for honeymooners."

It was a full day's tour, and I was glad we had not driven it ourselves. The small van we were in had nail-biting moments where I could see straight down the cliff beside us. If the driver sneezed, we would have gone over. Having to stop before every turn to allow another car to pass was often a narrow escape.

All the while, Freece was taking snapshots of every flower we passed, each dirt road, and palms that stood miles above us. The views that he captured on his camera were breathtaking, and he was eager to show me each shot.

"Shot 286. Only 800 to go," he announced with a quick bounce of his eyebrows.

He knows how those dancing brows get to me.

The tour bus made frequent stops along the lush rainforest, inviting us to step out and immerse ourselves in the vibrant surroundings. As we strolled hand in hand, our eyes would meet, exchanging knowing glances accompanied by playful winks. The warmth of our connection was palpable, prompting me to draw him closer for a tight embrace. In those tender moments, he never missed a chance to lean in, leaving soft kisses on my lips. The sheer bliss of it all made me want a lifetime of these affectionate moments.

"I love you more!" His words filled the air.

I couldn't help but smile. "I didn't even say anything."

"No, but you're thinking it," he whispered.

Suppressing our laughter, we wondered if those around us could sense the electric excitement of our honeymoon.

The rest of our week was amazing. We enjoyed the activities of the island snorkeling and floating together in the Pacific, surrounded only by the blue water and the creatures beneath us. The boat ride back to the hotel veered off course so we could capture photos of the dolphins and whales in the distance. On one of our last days, we stopped along the way to take more pictures of Black Rock Falls and for a ride to the top of the dormant volcano in Haleakala National Park. On the other side of the island, we stopped for dinner at Mama's Fish House. There, we enjoyed more sights and sounds of peaceful Maui.

On our last morning, we were off to the airport for another full day of travel back to Florida.

Despite my love for Florida's weather and beach views, Hawaii's are even more impressive.

Freece began unpacking his luggage.

"Did you unpack all the bags?"

"No, not yet. But I will. Mama and Rico are going to be here with Freddy soon."

That evening, I emptied my last bag and passed out the trinkets of souvenirs we had picked up along our journeys.

It was then that Freece asked, "What did you do with the camera? I want to show your mom some pictures we took."

"I did nothing with the camera. You've had it around your neck the whole trip."

"Well, not today; while we were traveling, I put it in its case. But look …" he said, holding the open camera case.

Inside the camera case was banana nut bread. No camera!

"Are you sure you put it inside the case? Because we bought banana bread three days ago," I said.

And there, we backtracked in our memory of all the places we had been these past few days, which led us to buying the banana nut bread.

"I put the bread in the case while we were walking so that it would keep shape. The only thing I can think of is the time we opened the trunk of the car to change our shoes to hike the black rock trails. I may have left the camera on the back fender of the car and never noticed. It's probably sitting in their parking lot," he said.

I called the airport, the hotel, and even Mama's Fish House, and none had seen our camera. So we had about 74 photos that I had taken with my cell phone. Flowers, trails, Black Rock cliff, and the drop off. Where I was sure the driver would slip over the edge, I had taken 20 photos to have proof in case of my death. And about 50 pictures of Freece.

He walked along the black rock beach and mockingly reached out his arms like the banyan tree. I had a few where he sat by the Pacific shore, gazing at the sky, wearing only his shorts and sunglasses. My favorite was the first morning of our honeymoon. Freece walked through the airport with the camera up to his face, taking a picture of me.

I printed 62 pictures and deleted the others. They were random selfies of me and blurred snaps from pushing the wrong button. Hence why Freece always carried the camera, and I never did.

We vowed never to buy banana bread again. No matter how good it tasted.

Part Ten

Parenthood

LITTLE BIT

Mama had maintained a relationship with Ms. Millie and Mr. Tim through the years. She would send a Christmas card and a letter about how we were doing. I would have loved for Mr. Tim to be the one to walk me down the aisle. But I knew his health was not good. When Mama last spoke to them, I had just had Freddy. Ms. Millie shared that Mr. Tim's health had declined.

"Ay, Vivian, I spoke to Ms. Millie, and she told me that Mr. Tim has died. She wanted to let us know the funeral is tomorrow."

My earliest memories of Mr. Tim go back to preschool. Mama had pictures of me with them as a baby. There were days I would run over to his house to watch him work in the garden or on his truck. I also spent time with Ms. Millie as she baked brownies and cookies.

Mr. Tim, in his dirty overalls and plaid shirt, always wore a hat to cover his tanned, weathered face. His brown eyes were old and wrinkled, and he had thin lips and skinny ears. He spoke with a twang in his voice. He looked at me with kindness and a sweet smile that brought the wrinkles upward on his cheeks. While he was a more handsome man in his younger years, my memory of him will always be what a kind and true soft-hearted man should be.

They moved away from Carroll Pines in the late 1990s to be closer to their children and to watch their grandchildren grow up in Plant City.

When we walked in, I didn't recognize anyone until their grandson came over.

"Vivi, you may not remember me. We used to play together when I would go to Grandpa Tim's house," he said.

I knew who he was. "Caleb! It has been a long time. I'm sorry for your loss and that this is how we're reconnecting," I said.

"Yeah, it's hard to believe that he's gone. You know he had lung cancer, and although he quit smoking, it was still not enough. Grandpa Tim spoke of you through the years," he said.

"I should have stayed connected with him. Not sure why I didn't. Your grandpa meant a lot to me growing up. He was my best friend for many years."

Mama saw familiar faces. She and Rico walked away while Caleb and I walked toward the casket. I tried not to look inside; I searched for Ms. Millie instead.

Then I realized the lady sitting in a wheelchair beside the coffin was her. She was small and frail. Her hair was white as snow, and her face was pale. She looked pretty, with her signature rosy-red cheeks and lipstick to match. I could tell she put her makeup on herself. She always enjoyed wearing makeup. She would use her red lipstick to touch her cheeks and blend a circle of rosy color to her face. Her blue eyes still gleamed and showed her gentleness, like Tim's. That was what they both had in common. Gentle and sweet.

She recognized me right away and reached out her arms to me.

"Hey there, Little Bit. You come here and let me hug you," she said.

She had a warm hug and a soft shoulder on which I rested my head, and her arms pulled me in like a soft pillow. I cried on her shoulder. She lifted my face.

"You're alright; Timothy is in heaven now, growing a garden for God," she said.

I smiled. She smiled.

I stood up and looked inside the casket. There he was. Mr. Tim wore a brown suit with a blue and tan striped tie. He was not wearing a hat and had his hair combed. His face looked clean. The lines on his face were now deeper, the wrinkles in the same places I remembered. His hands were lying on his stomach.

I had not seen him since I was 12 years old, and here I was 20 years later, and he had not changed.

After the funeral, I recognized a few faces; Mr. Cates and others from Willowdale Road were there. Mama and Rico were visiting and talking with those from the neighborhood. She had a lot to update them on since Daddy's funeral and my moving away to North Carolina.

Caleb invited us to go to Ms. Millie's house for lunch after the funeral. She had something for me at home. Mama and Rico chose not to go to Ms. Millie's.

Plant City was an old town east of Tampa. In the springtime, they had a Strawberry Festival with carnival rides, food vendors, games, and strawberry shortcake. Caleb reminded me that his Grandpa Tim took us to the festival when we were kids. I had forgotten that. That was the spring that Daddy died. Mr. Tim and Ms. Millie took me to their property in Plant City, where they parked an RV where their son Ronnie lived. Ronnie was Caleb's dad.

After the service, I drove to their home where we continued the memories and sat looking through photos of our time passed. Ms. Millie had me wheel her chair into the "doll room" where she had a collection of over fifty dolls. She handed me a beauty with long brown hair, hazel eyes, and long skinny legs.

"Timothy would always call this one Little Bit. The year he bought her was when you moved away. He wanted you to have her. I hope you take care of her," she said.

I held her close.

"Yes, of course. She looks like me." I laughed.

Ms. Millie laughed. "You and she are about the same height, too."

We both laughed.

"Timothy loved getting your letters when you lived up north with William. He would giggle and shed a tear just reading those letters. Vivian, he loved you," she said. "They diagnosed him with lung cancer five years after you moved away. He had treatments, and that paused the cancer for a little while. But it always came back," she continued. "He sometimes asked me, 'I wonder what happened to that little bitty girl from next door?'"

Then she reached over, grabbed my hand, and leaned in. She asked if I remembered the boy who lived on the back property, the Taylor boy.

"I do. I remember he passed away from cancer, too," I said.

Ms. Millie went on, "Yes, he died of cancer. He never wanted the treatments. We would go by his house to bring his pain medication and sometimes take him to doctor appointments. But he told Timothy that he wanted to die in the home that he had built. He wanted to die with no pain during his sleep." She continued her story, "On the day Tim and I found the Taylor boy in his house, we were out in the garden pulling vegetables. That's when we saw two girls sprinting away from his place." Her eyes gazed into mine, and she lowered her head and lifted her brows.

"The Taylor boy wanted to die in his home. He didn't want cancer treatments, surgeries, hospitals, or doctors poking at him. So, God heard his prayer and allowed him to have peace. Tim and I always wondered if you knew that was what the Taylor boy wanted?" she asked.

A little shaken, I replied, "No. I didn't know that. But I am glad he could die peacefully in his home without pain."

And it was there that I realized that she knew. It was me and Shannon who found him dead. And we were the ones who placed the rock in front of the door. It was Mr. Tim and Ms. Millie who had been giving Cliff Taylor his pain medication. When they saw us running from the house, they knew they had to be the ones to find him next. They removed the rock and called in for the body to be collected.

I spent the rest of the day enjoying our conversations about Tim with his family. They shared memories of the house on Willowdale Road. Ms. Millie told a story that I had forgotten about me taking a washer I had found on the ground and wearing it like a ring. I noticed it was too tight on my finger the next day, so I showed Tim. He saw that it was the washer from a screw he was missing while working on his truck. He took wire cutters and slowly clipped; he was careful not to cut me.

On my drive home, I called Freece and shared my day with him. I was thankful he could stay with Freddy while I said my goodbyes to my dear friend.

It was a beautiful day as I drove home and thought about Mr. Tim. I could hear his voice now. *Good night, Little Bit. Get home safe.*

JANUARY

Having a best friend who stayed with you from childhood through adulthood was rare.

Shannon and I had years go by after I moved away from her family's home in North Carolina, where we didn't speak at all. The year I started using social media, I took a chance and looked her up.

After messaging and exchanging phone numbers, we got together and visited. We lived in neighboring cities and met at the sponge docks in Tarpon Springs.

Shannon and her husband, Nicholas, were already there when we arrived. She looked the same. Hearing her voice and feeling her presence brought me back to being a kid again.

The four of us sat down to lunch while she and I went on and on about our childhood, right up to the year I moved away. I told her about Mr. Tim's passing and about the story that Ms. Millie had told of finding Cliff Taylor that day. We both shared the story of our secret pact with Nicholas and Freece. Although the scar on my hand was light and thin now, we both knew it was there.

It was then that I learned of her dad's passing a few years back when he was in a work-related accident. William had stayed on the mountain and married Darla. Her mom, Wanda, lived in Tampa after the divorce, and she remarried and moved to Sarasota, Florida.

We laughed, promised to keep in touch, and stayed true to our promise through the years to follow. New Year's celebrations and fireworks on the Fourth of July were traditions we've continued since. She and Nicholas had twin boys a few years younger than Freddy.

Shannon and I continued to text and call on birthdays and holidays.

I was proud that we stayed true to our "blood sister pact" and kept our secret until the day we shared it with our husbands. It was in those moments that I was reassured that we'd always have one another to confide in, no matter where we were in our lives. I cherished her presence and the comfort she gave me. I knew she would be there if I ever needed her in a time of stress.

It's My Life

It was true; I had been in love more than once. True love, twice. But there was nothing I could compare the love for my son to. As time passed and Freddy grew older, we all forgot about the things we should have told him. Instead, we focused on the busyness of our lives.

After Freece and I were married, Freddy and I moved to St. Pete to live with Freece in his home. It wasn't until the year Freddy started school that we began looking for a larger home to buy. Although we found many options in St. Pete and Tampa, being near Mama and Liv was important. But the final decision came down to the school district.

It was right after dinner that Freece and I discussed having more children. Freddy had been asking for a brother or sister.

"Have you thought about us having a child now?"

"To be honest, having Freddy is everything to me. Having more was never something I needed or gave much thought to." Freece paused. "If it happens, then, of course, I would love that."

"I feel the same. Having Freddy has always been enough for me. But I want to be fair to you." I said in a whisper, still careful that Freddy wouldn't hear me. And aware that Freece may want a child *of his own.*

We both agreed. If it happened, it would happen.

Carroll Pines was still a special place for me. Through the years, it had changed. What was once a small town of cow pastures and orange groves had become a small sub-city in North Tampa. The area had grown over the years and built a new elementary, middle, and high school. What Freece liked most about the high school was that it offered an Academy of Information Technology.

"Even if Freddy doesn't pursue IT as a career, it would still be beneficial for him to take the classes and learn from the experience," Freece said.

Over the years, Freddy was active in the local baseball and basketball leagues. One year, he tried out for the hockey team but found it too aggressive and fast-paced. I was glad about that, not having to worry that each game would be the one where his teeth would get knocked out.

So, when he made the marching band in high school, I was thrilled that sports were behind him and that we could still attend Friday night football games with him. He was active in school, and we all enjoyed watching him grow.

Even so, that underlying secret was there, and still the worst part was that we never told Freddy.

The social networks mostly used by teenagers were not just for reconnecting with old friends, as I had done with Shannon. It wasn't until my son was leaving for college that I began posting to my page.

"This will be a good way for you and me to stay in touch. And I can post things I'm doing at school. You and Dad can stay connected too by posting for me to see," Freddy suggested, as he updated the app to my phone.

He had always been a good kid—responsible, talented, innovative, and kind. He was the one who took the Golden Rule to heart. Freddy was considerate to everyone he met. When he requested to be "friends," I accepted. I updated my profile photo to one of us on his first day of college. It was the day I let him go.

We were not prepared for the day we had to leave our child at college for the first time. Through the years, Freddy had gone to summer camp since he was in seventh grade. I was always excited to take him to school as all the kids got on the bus and drove out of state to stay with strangers in a city we had never been to. Their chaperones were the "cool teachers" that you hoped would keep an eye on your son above the others.

A few weeks later, they would return and share the stories of how much fun they had and the work they did. He would finish each year with, "I can't wait to go again next year."

The first day of college was the same routine for everyone. The parents showed up with a truckload of furniture, boxes, and bins full of things their child never wanted. Dads carried boxes up and down the elevator, and moms put an entire dorm room together in three hours. We did this not because our child wanted it but because, if we were honest, our child would prefer us to drop them at the door so they could handle it all themselves. But they let us. They allowed us to do it all. They seemed to know that this moment was not about them. It was our last day to be a part of their world.

Parents came prepared to make the dorm rooms as comfortable as home. They believed placing an area rug and sofa towards the television, with new linens and a distinctive shower curtain, would showcase their child's uniqueness.

And then it was time to leave him. I remembered saying goodbye and giving Freddy a hug and a quick kiss on his cheek. His dad scooped him up as much as he could carry him for a hug and a kiss.

"Come on, Dad!" He squirmed.

"Yes. You may be going to college, but I am still your dad, and you are still my boy," Freece said.

We stepped away and took in a good glance.

He hurried us. "I gotta go! They're starting the welcome activities."

And off he went to change the world.

I got in the car, and the tears had already started. I looked over, and Freece was wiping away a flood he had hidden until now. We waited a few more minutes in the car, hoping he would run back and say he didn't want to go to college. What was that pain called? That ache you felt as you watched your son run away towards friends. Towards school. Towards his future. You realized that this experience did not include you at the moment. You wouldn't be in his life for the next four years. He was deciding for himself, and that was when I accepted it. This was not about me. This was his moment to shine.

"Today is the day we trust he remembers all that we taught him and will use it here on his own," I said.

And his dad looked over at me.

"I know. I only wish I could do it with him."

And there it began for us as we searched for a place to get a glass of wine and have an early dinner. Alone.

We considered all the great times Freddy would have, the girls he would date, or even find his wife there. It was an enjoyable day, allowing us time to let him go. He was ready.

We were not.

Part Eleven

Death

VIVIAN'S SECRET

I loved every day with Freece. I could not imagine any person I would rather be with. We raised Freddy together and had beautiful memories to keep and share. There was still one thing I held inside: my secret. I could not seem to let it go. There was this ache inside me. I imagined Freddy's father wanting a life with him one day.

In previous years, I clung to Danny's words and hoped he would have wanted a child. I could tell him *we have a son.* I stopped myself from thinking about that. Because I was reminded of the many times he said, *Children are not something I want, and I would only screw them up like my father did to me.*

While Liv searched for Billy Miller on social media, I was there.

"Carter, look at this guy. This was my first husband, Billy Miller," Liv said.

I watched her type in the name and the city, and there he was. He was married with three children and looked better now that he was older.

Thursday nights had become a night where Freece and I would do something independently. He had joined a men's hockey league, and I joined a weekly book club. We had a day off because some of the ladies were out of town. It was then, while I was alone, I searched for Daniel Bullet, North Carolina, on social media. And there he was: Dan Bullet.

We were not "friends", so I couldn't see his profile. I couldn't tell if he was married or had children. I didn't want to be friends, so I

sent a private message to him.
Messenger:
Me: Hey stranger, remember me?

I typed and waited. I was so nervous and began pacing around the house.

What was I thinking? I should delete it.

I opened Messenger, and there was a notification pending. He had read it. I couldn't delete it now. *Oh God. Now, what did I do?*

I opened it.

Danny: Of course I remember you. I could never forget you. How have you been?

Me: I am doing good. This messenger is a terrific way to reunite. I live in Carroll Pines still. My son Freddy graduated from college last year and got married this year. He and Elizabeth live nearby too. How about you? Did you ever get married or have kids?

… He was typing.

Danny: No. I never had kids. I got married, but she passed away from breast cancer. After retiring from the military, I moved back home to care for my mom and dad. One of my old girlfriends, Lauren, and I reunited and got married. Seven years later, she passed away. It's good to hear about Freddy. But what about you?

Me: Yes, I'm married, but Freddy is my only child.

Danny: Well, Vivi, that is good to hear. I am happy you settled down and had everything you wanted. So good to hear from you again. Don't be a stranger.

Me: You too. Good to talk again.

That evening, Freece came in from his hockey game.

"I'm going to take a quick shower before I have dinner."

I followed him into the bathroom. "Remember the man I told you was Freddy's father, Danny Bullet?" I began.

"Yeah, I remember. What happened?" he said, turning on the shower.

I raised my voice over the sounds. "No. Nothing happened. But I found him on social media today, and I messaged him."

"Did you *tell* him?"

"No. I thought about it. But I know if we decided to tell anyone, we should tell Freddy first," I said, putting his clothes into the laundry basket.

With his voice raised, Freece replied, "Yeah, the first person *should be* Freddy. But I don't know if we should ever tell him. That news will be hard for him to take, especially after all these years. What good would come of it? It could only lead to more problems."

I could hear his adamant tone; clearly, he had been thinking about this and weighing the decision for some time. I stepped out of the bathroom and waited on the bed for Freece, contemplating the situation and whether it was right for me to keep this from Freddy any longer.

And now, I have to consider Freece's feelings too.

I heard the shower turned off.

"I'm not saying I want to tell him, but help me see the reasons we shouldn't?"

"Do you think any good can come out of it? Personally, I think it will cause more problems than good," he replied.

I wanted to do what was best for Freddy, now that he was an adult. Still, I struggled with the consequences of hurting him. It was no longer about Freddy and *a father*. This was more about *a secret and trust* that I feared could be lost.

Danny could be a great man in Freddy's life. It should be Freddy's decision. He and Freddy could have a connection and that wasn't lost on me. And still the obvious pain hiding inside was how Freddy would feel towards me now. Knowing I had kept this secret for so long when our relationship had seemed so perfect.

"So, we both agree. Don't tell him?" I confirmed.

"I think so, Vivi. I wouldn't tell him. Besides, I don't think I'm ready for that," Freece admitted.

Me either.

"Maybe we write a letter and leave it to Freddy, for when we both are gone?" Freece suggested.

Neither of us were ready to face the truth. To face what we should have done sooner. Time would certainly tell.

"Yeah, I like that. I'll write the letter," I said, as I went to the kitchen to heat dinner.

April Showers Bring May Flowers

The city of Savannah truly can bring that phrase to life.

Springtime in Savannah, Georgia, was beautiful. In Savannah, the streets burst with strawberry blossoms, and pink azaleas adorn the Squares. I visited there over the years, and I loved that town. It had so much history. Walking the streets of Savannah, you could feel the change in time. The brick and stone gave the roads a nostalgic feeling. You could hear the horse carriages and the sounds of their shoes galloping along the hard street. The trolley chimed as you took through the squares with the canopy of trees and Spanish moss dripping over.

They had renovated the mansions and buildings of their past. Massive stairwells extended from the front door, reaching towards the sky of the house.

Similar to Florida, the weather in Savannah lacked heavy humidity. The heat was there with a gentle breeze from a nearby river.

If you liked the crowds and green beer, March was an exciting time to visit Savannah. Throughout the month, patrons walked and drank to celebrate Saint Patrick's Day. It could get wild, not to mention the traffic was horrendous. Too much for me.

I opened the soft pink envelope and read that Carmen and Marc's wedding would be in April.

"Hey, Freece. Guess who is having a destination wedding in Savannah, Georgia?"

"I give up. Tell me who!"

"Marc and Carmen. They sent us this beautiful invite. It looks like it will be a small, intimate wedding. We should go, we could drive there," I said.

"Sure, let's do it. It would only be about five to six hours' driving."

"Great, I'll call her and let her know before I send the RSVP."

So, I planned our trip.

"I can make dinner reservations at the Olde Pink House; there's so much history there. We can tour some historical homes, and the trolley bus gives a great tour. And did you ever read the book *Midnight in the Garden of Good and Evil?* That was about Savannah. Oh wow! We're going to have so much fun," I said to Freece excitedly.

His only response was, "I can't believe we've never been there together."

"I have known Carmen Ward since we were kids. We share memories of swimming and fishing from her dock. She inherited the house on the lake after her parents passed away. That's when she renovated it. Marc was the contractor that worked for her father's company, and the reason she never sold it. He put too much work into it," I said.

Freece hugged me and said, "I'm excited to go to a destination wedding in a historical city. What could be better?"

After I confirmed our reservations at the River Street Inn. I shared with Freece, "The outside can be deceiving with the old rusty brick, but once you step inside, the spiral staircase is spectacular, and each room is a gem of time."

We were excited to get away, to a beautiful city, while we watched Carmen and Marc get married.

What could go wrong?

A Moment in Time

The rain was coming down so thick and heavy. It was the loud rain, which gave a *pang, pang, pang* with each drop hitting the windshield.

"Freece, are you good, hun? Do you want to pull over?" I asked.

"No, we should be fine if we can get through this heavy section. You know rain only lasts 15 minutes," he said.

"I am glad the rain didn't ruin Marc and Carmen's wedding. It was beautiful."

I kept the conversation going while we navigated the storm. He was leaning forward and wiping the windshield with his hand. I fidgeted with the defrost buttons which cleared the windshield. And just then I got a notification from Messenger. I opened the phone to read …

And that was the moment my life stopped.

Everything happened so fast. I looked up from my phone and saw the headlights approaching us. I closed my eyes and felt the car slide. We were spinning, and then everything moved slowly.

My eyes were open.

My eyes were closed.

I heard a scream and felt the crash.

The car continued to spin and flip …

I'm awake.
The lights are so bright. I am alone in the room. Why can't I move my head? Only my eyes, darting back and forth. I am trying to talk, but my mouth is full. I cannot swallow.
Hello! Is anyone here with me? Can you see me? I'm awake. Am I talking, or am I saying this in my mind?

I passed out.

My eyes won't open, and I hear voices.

I passed out again.

Part Twelve

Forgiveness

A Son's Secret

Freddy

Elizabeth and I rushed into mom's hospital room. She was in the Intensive Care Unit. They were keeping her stabilized with medication. She looked … broken. Her face and hands were swollen and there were tubes everywhere. They allowed me to sit with her.

"Mom. Mom! It's me, Freddy. Can you hear me?" I begged.

There was no response; she just laid there.

Day 2

Mom always prayed at times like these. I prayed for her now. *Dear God, please...*

The nurses came in again and checked her vital signs. They are keeping her elevated, because her heart rate would rise and cause her to have convulsions each time she laid flat. They asked me if I knew of any heart conditions from the past.

Day 3

When I arrived, they explained that they medically induced her into a coma. She was on a ventilator that made her look so frail. I never thought I'd see my mom with tubes in her nose and down her throat. They were able to do X-rays and an MRI.

"It only looks worse than it is; this is best for her heart," the nurse said.

I planned to go to her place tonight and check her file cabinets. She always told me she kept her medical records and important papers there.

I drove home from Mom's house and sat in the driveway, not ready to go inside and face Elizabeth. I wiped my face, but the tears kept coming. The pain, the tears, the anger. *How come she never told me?*

The comforting smell of Elizabeth's cooking filled the air as I stepped inside. Pasta and sauce. She was standing at the stove and turned toward me.

"Hey babe. How's your mom?" Elizabeth asked.

I rushed towards her, wrapped my arms around her tightly, unable to hold back my tears.

"Oh Freddy. What happened? What did the doctor say today?"

She thought I was crying and hurting because of Mom's condition; she doesn't see the letter I'm holding. I pulled away from her and lifted my hand.

"I went by Mom's place to see if she had any family history of medical issues, and I found this …"

She looked at me and back at the letter.

Freddy, My Love,

I have written this letter a thousand times and know that I have loved you always.

Your biological father's name is Daniel Robert Bullet. He lives in Spring Mountain Valley, North Carolina. It is a small town, so you should be able to find him. He knew I had a son; he just never knew that you were his son. Freece and I decided never to tell you. The fear of you hating me and leaving me was too much. I know I was selfish. As a young mother, I was alone. Danny never wanted to marry me. We were in love, but he had a career in the military that took him all over the world. Danny never wanted a family or marriage.

When I met Freece, we fell in love and he wanted to marry me. He fell in love with you, too. He took us both as his family. The three of us were happy together. There was no reason to change what we had.

Find him. He should have the chance to get to know you. And you deserve the opportunity to know your father.

I love you, my son. Always, Mom

Elizabeth gasped. "Oh my, Freddy! I can't believe this."
We both stood there in silence.

I wanted to call Abuela Sofia and Abuelo Rico because I knew they wouldn't lie if I confronted them, but I didn't know if they knew. So, I called Aunt Liv instead.

"Hey, Freddy. We planned to go to the hospital tonight and visit Vivi. Abuela called and told us they placed her in a medically induced coma," Liv responded.

I went into the closet, removed my shoes, and had to step out in order for my cell service to be clear. I could barely hear her. I was feeling frantic and angry that I couldn't help but pace back and forth. She kept talking.

"You know how strong your mom is. She'll get through this."

I stepped into the living room. My voice echoed.

"How long have you known?" I finally asked. I was pissed. My voice was firm. I had someone to yell at, and Liv was the one person who would know mom's secrets.

"I'm sorry, what? What happened?" she stammered.

"How. Long. Have. You. Known?" I demanded. *She was going to make me say it.*

"How long have you known that Freece was not my father? And who the hell is Dan Bullet? Don't lie to me, Aunt Liv. I cannot take any more lies," I said, my hands shaking.

"Let's meet and talk," she said.

There, she doesn't deny it. I hoped she would.

"No. I don't want to meet. I want to hear everything right now. Tell me."

"Okay, Freddy, I don't know if I can. This is something your mom and dad should have told you. How did you find out?"

I overheard Uncle Carter talking in the background. She had me on speakerphone. "Just tell him since his mom can't."

"Okay, yes. Everything you're saying is the truth. I'm so sorry, but you're right, Freece isn't your biological father. His name is

Daniel Bullet. He was your mother's childhood boyfriend from North Carolina, and they reunited in Tampa when he was in the Air Force," Liv confessed.

"They met when Mom lived with William and Shannon? She was a kid back then," I said, wrapping my head around this.

"Yeah, and then five years later, he unexpectedly ran into her at the beach during his time at MacDill. Your mom called him Danny. We never met him; he kept himself private, and when he told her he only wanted to be friends and never wanted to marry or have children, she believed him. Vivi was only eighteen when they started dating; you were born soon afterward."

"He didn't want to meet me?" I asked.

"No, your mom invited him over to meet you, but that's when he got scared and realized Vivi was a mother, and he went on," she explained.

"You know, it was a year or two later that she met Freece. He loved you and spent time with you. I am so sorry, Freddy. How did you find out?"

"Mom wrote a letter to me. I found it with her important papers."

"See? She was planning to tell you. You have to believe that she never wanted to hurt you, and that letter proves it," Liv said.

Day 4

The doctors didn't see any change.

"In this state, we can keep her stabilized. We took chest X-rays and saw that she had broken ribs, but her organs are in good shape. We will continue to monitor her," the nurse relayed.

After work each day, I went to Mom's bedside. The nurse had my cell phone number and would call me immediately if there were any updates.

I called Elizabeth. "Today, they are seeing some improvement and have removed the ventilator. They plan to remove the medication that kept her in the coma. We may start seeing more changes tomorrow," I said, uncertain if I believed it, but doing all I could to hold it together and stay positive. This secret was killing me inside, but Mom's recovery was at the forefront of my mind.

In the early morning, I received a phone call.

"Your mom is awake, and she's looking for you. When I mentioned your name, her eyes lit up," Nurse Kate said.

I arrived at the hospital early and stayed with her. Her eyes opened, and although her throat was sore when she swallowed, she spoke softly and sounded hoarse. She was weak, and her body was aching. But she was alive.

With tears streaming down her face, Mom asked about Freece and gazed at me. She knew.

She mouthed the words, "Is he dead?"

I nodded and said firmly, "Yes."

I held her while we both cried. She was so small in my arms. I felt her pain as she realized her best friend, lover, husband, and greatest confidant was gone. It was then that I was able to fall apart as well. The realization that my dad, my father, the man I loved for as far back as my memories could go, was gone.

At that moment, I was not mad at her and knew that my day of anger would soon come.

Four days later, they released Mom to come home. The doctor felt that she was strong enough now to leave the hospital, and she had been asking each day to go. We still had not had the funeral for Freece. I called Elizabeth.

"Mom is coming home, but they recommend she not be alone still. We'll see you soon," I said.

"Are you going to bring up the letter? You should wait," Elizabeth cautioned.

Not wanting Mom to know our conversation, I hinted to Elizabeth.

"Not now, but later. They are getting a wheelchair for her, and we can talk when we are all together. See you, babe," and hung up the phone. I had no intention of bringing up the letter. I would when the time was right.

The following week, we had Dad's funeral.

Goodbye, Dad

Freddy

Freece Lee Miles died on Sunday, April 16, 2017.

He is survived by his wife, Vivian Miles and son Frederick Miles, and daughter-in-law Elizabeth of Carroll Pines, Florida.

"She's doing okay, but doesn't want to eat," Elizabeth said.

"I know. For now, just let her sit near him. We can eat once we're home," I said.

I stood near the doorway, greeting everyone as they came in. Mom sat in a chair next to the open casket. "He is still beautiful, even though I can't see his blue eyes," she said.

She stopped crying, but I'm unsure if she was just holding it together or had cried it all out. I was happy to see her friends, Carmen, and Shannon, were there beside her.

Mom asked me to speak at Dad's funeral. I didn't know what to say. The pastor suggested for me to, "Speak from your heart. Tell us a story of when your dad taught you a lesson."

I looked over at the crowd of people as they stared up at me.

"My dad, Freece, *was* ..." I stopped. My voice cracked and tears began. I cleared my throat, not knowing what to say.

"My dad was from New York. After finishing college, he moved to Florida on his own. Although he loved New York, he loved the warm weather more. He was the type of man who worked smart, not hard. He was a brilliant man who liked to read and work with his hands. Once, he needed electrical work done in the house. He read a book on electrical rewiring and when he called the electrician to come out, he told him he didn't need him to do the work but asked him to inspect what he had done. That guy told Dad, 'You did a great job; you sure you don't want to come work for me?'"

There were laughs across the crowd. It felt good to smile and share the story. "Dad told him, 'No, I could never charge as much as you do.' He later told me he only spent fifty bucks after buying the supplies and doing the work himself."

"Dad taught me three things I remember most: 'one, never let another person tell you what you are worth. Two, do the work yourself, and you'll be proud of it when you're done.
And three, you can't learn everything by reading a book.' My dad taught me kindness."

After the funeral, we headed back to our house. I was driving, with mom and Elizabeth in the car, and the radio played *Wake Me Up When September Ends* by Green Day, and I couldn't stop the tears.

I always thought of Freece as my father. My last name was the same as his: Miles. My earliest memories are filled with him in my life. He called me son; I called him dad. It was not until I read that letter that I realized he and Mom had lied. I was angry and hurt by them both. But that night in the hospital, I felt scared that I would lose them both. I have forgiven them, and I have come to understand their decisions more.

Mom returned to our house after we left the hospital. We arranged the guest room near the kitchen for her. Having Abuela Sofia and Abuelo Rico there each day with her was nice. They visited in the mornings and stayed all day with her. They took her to the doctor appointments, freeing Elizabeth, and me to resume work. This gave her and Abuela the time they needed. Abuela enjoyed taking care of her daughter again; Elizabeth and I enjoyed coming home to Abuela's cooked meals each night. After dinner, we walked around the neighborhood. Mom was slowly rebuilding her energy and strength. She began eating more and was looking healthy again. There was something still and quiet about her. That vibrant zeal was gone. I wondered if she would be this way forever.

One evening after dinner, Mom spoke up and said, "I'm ready to go back home."

FRESH SALTY AIR

Vivi

I was glad to be home. It took a while to adjust, walking around the house, seeing Freece's things, and feeling his presence despite his absence. I'm still not completely comfortable without him. I expect him to walk in the front door.

The mornings were the toughest as I sat with my cup of coffee, staring out the window, thinking of him. *He used to make my coffee for me.* Each morning started with tears and an emptiness that didn't go away. Taking walks and finding things to do helped. But none of that was for sure healing. Time. That's what I needed. Time to pass.

A month had passed since Freece's funeral. My heart was still raw from the pain of losing him. I never wanted that pain to heal, afraid that I would forget him.

Each morning, I practiced yoga and stretched my body. The exercise gave me the motivation and energy to get through the day. Most days, I was sad and lonely. Our wedding and vacation photos filled the house. I walked around, talking to him like he was in the next room. He still gave me comfort.

I called Freddy.

"Hey Freddy, how are you doing today? It's beautiful outside. Would you and Elizabeth like to go to dinner near the beach?" I asked.

"You sound better," he said.

"I am ready to walk and get some fresh, salty air."

"Sure. We were thinking of calling you, too. The beach sounds good," Freddy agreed.

"I'll drive and pick you both up around 4:30. I know a fun spot for dinner."

We drove over Howard Frankland Bridge and headed towards a quieter place. It was still one of my favorite drives. At any time of day, the sun's reflection on the water reminded me of a floating candle.

"I always played games with Freddy while crossing this bridge when he was little. How many boats can you see? How many jet skis do you see? Any sailboats or kayaks? And he would stretch himself to see out the window to begin his count."

"I remember that." Freddy smiled.

"Elizabeth, do you see any boats?" I joked.

Madeira Beach was perfect for a peaceful evening. We arrived at Beach Bayou a little after six o'clock.

"I have been coming here for years, since high school," I said.

We walked to an open table where the views were the best. The water was busy that day, and the beaches were filled with the seagulls squawking as they sought an unsuspecting kid who might drop a French fry.

We began with wine and Freddy selected two appetizers. We continued our lovely dinner, discussing their plans to begin a family. Elizabeth was doing well in her position and felt she had the time to take off work to have a baby soon.

"That is the best news I have heard in a long time. Thank you for that. The two of you will be amazing parents," I said.

Tension was in the air. I felt it; they felt it. Freddy was quiet. He spoke with a quick reply to anything said. Elizabeth started the conversation and was the first to comment when I spoke. I wanted to ask them if everything was okay. But I knew the answer to that. I could hear in my mind, *No, Mom. Everything is not okay. It is not okay that you have kept my father from me all these years.* So, I didn't ask the obvious. It was too late for that.

Before the server took my credit card, I said, "I'd like to take a walk on the beach; I want to tell you something."

I slipped off my sandals, and we walked toward the water. The sand was warm and soft as we walked down to the beach where it blended with a cool touch of wet sand, where the waves cooled the shore. My footprints disappeared. We walked. They held hands and giggled together as they splashed with salty taps on the shoreline. I noticed the perfect spot up ahead and laid out the blanket that I'd brought along for this moment. I had always carried a blanket and extra towels in the trunk of my car. It truly was a necessity when living near the beaches.

I paused, looking up and down the beach line choosing a spot out of earshot of others. I wish I had wine to survive this conversation. They both sat down and seemed to know what I was about to tell them. I felt it.

"The sky is beautiful tonight," Elizabeth said, softening the moment.

I took a deep breath, steeled my nerves, and began. "Freddy, I need to talk to you. Please let me finish before you respond. I owe this to you." I told him everything. From meeting Danny in school in North Carolina to our first kiss behind the bus.

"I thought I'd never see Danny again after I moved from North Carolina."

Freddy took a moment to look over at me. I couldn't tell if he was angry or listening with intent.

I continued. "Once we were reunited in Tampa, we spent all our nights at the Surfside Inn or the Base Hotel, where we began our love story. Until I discovered I was pregnant, I lived a lie." I stopped. I wanted to see his reaction. He gave none. "My fear was that Danny would reject you, too. I was a kid myself, having a baby. I was making decisions, and I didn't know if they were right or wrong. After I met Freece, he met you and loved you immediately. He treated you like a son. I saw only that, and we were a family."

With tears rolling down my face, I continued. I felt guilty for my tears. It wasn't my moment. I tried to look into Freddy's eyes, but he kept his face down.

"After your marriage to Elizabeth, I spoke with Freece, and we both agreed that it was too late to tell you. That's when we decided I would write a letter to you. Which I hoped you would find, along with my Final Will, someday when we both had passed. Only after I left the hospital did the nurse call to follow up a few days later. She asked me how I was doing and told me. 'Your son was so smart to search for your medical history.'"

I didn't want him to stop me with questions. I pressed on. "When I checked the filing cabinet, I noticed the letter was gone. I'm glad you found it. Now you know, and it wouldn't surprise me if you never spoke to me again. Danny is alive, and last I heard, he is back in North Carolina." I stopped.

Freddy looked up. Tears rolled down his face. I handed him a towel to wipe his eyes. Elizabeth gazed at the sky and then wiped her eyes.

"How do you know he's alive and lives in North Carolina? Have you talked to him?"

"No. No. I never had the chance to talk to him. We had planned to meet in Charleston, but Danny couldn't."

Freddy's eyes held a deep sadness as he looked over at me. I could see his pain.

"Mom, I have so many things running through my mind. Yes, I read the letter. I have known about Danny for a month now. When I first read it, you were still in the hospital and not stable enough to talk or listen. So Elizabeth and I dealt with this pain. I've spent a lot of time contemplating everything. My emotions towards you and dad are a mix of feeling betrayed and empathy. I was still angry when I spoke to Aunt Liv, and she confirmed everything. It made me consider your perspective at 18. I had always known you didn't attend college because you had me. What if Danny had known about me then? He may have been able to help you, and you could have gone to college. We could have had a different life. But then, we may have never met Freece. I cannot picture my life without Freece as my dad. So, for that, I'm not mad. Just hurt. I'll need time, but we're fine," he said.

I looked up.

Staring into his eyes that mirrored mine, I saw a man. The most beautiful and forgiving man I could ever know.

"Can I hug you?" I said in my blubbery mess.

"Of course, Mom. I'm still your son."

Ah! His words filled my heart.

Elizabeth and I leaned in on Freddy's shoulders, the three of us watching the sunset on the water. The day turned to gray gloom, and the sky's light had an amber glow. The night was coming to a start as the sounds of the soft waves rolled in and the chatter of families walking by as they enjoyed their night on vacation.

The sun was now hidden below the water.

"Should we go now?" Elizabeth asked.

"Let's get some ice cream first," Freddy suggested.

The Secret is Out

Vivi

The doorbell rang. I opened the door to Elizabeth.

"Hey there. I didn't know you were coming over today. Is everything okay?"

"I've wanted to talk to you alone for some time now. Freddy is with work friends tonight," she said, walking past me. She beeline toward the kitchen.

"Is everything good with you and Freddy?" I asked.

"Yeah, we're fine."

We moved to the kitchen, and she sat at the counter.

"Is this a glass of wine or a cup of coffee conversation?" I asked.

"A glass of wine would be good."

"Oh! You're making me nervous." I hurried to get the glasses and pour the wine.

She began, "On the beach, you mentioned to Freddy about Danny being his dad."

"Yeah, go on," I said.

"Well, I hoped you would've told Freddy the whole truth. But you didn't." She stopped.

"I'm confused, Elizabeth; what more can I tell him?" My brows turned down.

"You and Freece were taken to the hospital on the night of the accident. When we arrived, they handed me your belongings, including your purse, cell phone, and Freece's things. Freddy was too busy talking with the nurses and on the phone with Aunt Liv and Uncle Carter about Freece's status. I was holding your bag, and your cell phone kept vibrating."

I sipped my wine.

What was on my phone? I can't remember anything wrong.

"When I opened it, I saw you had three unread notifications. I'm sorry, but I read them all. I noticed you and Danny exchanged messages during the week of Marc and Carmen's wedding. You told Freddy that you had not talked to Danny," she said.

I looked at her in shock.

She asked, "Were you seeing Danny while you were with Freece?"

"No! I haven't seen Danny since before Freece and I were engaged." I caught myself raising my voice.

She insisted. "But I saw the messages. You were at the wedding in Savannah during that time. Just before the accident."

"Yes, Elizabeth, I messaged Danny to meet with us. I was asking him to meet with me AND Freece. But we never met up. Danny texted me, saying he was out of town that week and could not get together. So, we never told Danny about Freddy being his son. The messages that you read were after we received the wedding invitation. Freece came up with the idea for us to go to Charleston before the wedding and meet with Danny," I said.

Our conversation about whether we would tell Freddy now or in a letter for him to find at our death was one we'd had a thousand times.

One night, Freece made it all make sense:

"Let's consider whether we should tell Danny first that he has a son."

"What if he says, 'I don't want a son'?"

"Then nothing is lost."

"But if we tell Freddy first, and he reaches out to Danny, and he rejects him, then we have Freddy hurt by Danny and us. All is lost. Let's tell Danny first."

"I don't know why, but I fear he'll say, 'Yes, I want to meet my son.'"

"Then we can ask him not to say anything until you can talk to Freddy. Then the two of them can meet on their own terms."

"Elizabeth, I appreciate you looking out for Freddy. But please know, my intention has always been good."

"I just don't want Freddy to hurt anymore."

"You can look at my phone. You can view all the messages and texts."

I slid my phone to Elizabeth and showed her the entire conversation that me and Danny had on messenger.

Me: Hey stranger, remember me?

Dan Bullet: Of course I remember you. I'll never forget you. How have you been?

Me: I'm doing good. This messenger is a terrific way to reunite. I live in Carroll Pines still. My son Freddy graduated from college last year and got married this year. He and Elizabeth live nearby too. How about you? Did you ever get married or have kids?

Dan Bullet: No. I never had kids. I got married, but she passed away from breast cancer. After retiring from the military, I moved back home to care for my mom and dad. One of my old girlfriends, Lauren, and I reunited and got married. Seven years later, she passed away. It is good to hear about Freddy. But what about you?

Me: Yes, I am married, but Freddy is my only child.

Dan Bullet: Well, Vivi, that is good to hear. I'm happy you settled down and had everything you wanted. So good to hear from you again. Don't be a stranger.

Me: You too. Good to talk again.

Me: Hey Danny, would you like to meet up? We're going to a wedding in Savannah and could meet.

Dan Bullet: I would like that. It would be good to visit again.

Me: I'll let you know when we are in town.

Me: We are here in Charleston. Are you available to meet up?

Danny Bullet: Hey, I will be out of town this week. How long are you going to be in Charleston?

Me: We are here today. We leave tomorrow morning for a wedding in Savannah.

Danny Bullet: Damn! It would have been good to meet Freece and

catch up.
Me: Next time.

Danny Bullet: How was Savannah? Sorry, I missed you. I was thinking of going to Tampa for a military reunion at MacDill. Can we get together then?
Danny Bullet: Heavy rains are heading your way, stay safe.
Danny Bullet: Call me when you're back home.

"These last three text messages must have been the ones you saw after the accident. I can see how those came across. I never called or texted Danny back."

Part Thirteen

Family

Is Now a Good Time?

Vivi

Freddy messaged the only Dan Bullet in Mountain Springs Valley, North Carolina, using social media.

Freddy Miles: Hello. My name is Freddy. You may remember my mother, Vivian Perez Miles.

There was no response that day.

The next day, Freddy received a notification on messenger.

Dan Bullet: Yeah, I know Vivi. Is your mom okay?

Freddy Miles: Can I call you?

Dan Bullet: Sure.

The phone rang.

"Yeah, this is Dan."

Freddy asked his father, "Is now a good time?"

Danny shared his stories of meeting Vivi and his crush on her for the first time. His pride had prevented him from confessing before, but he couldn't let the opportunity slip away when he saw her at the beach five years later.

"I loved your mom right away. She was the most beautiful girl I knew. Her heart led me towards her."

"Why didn't you ever ask her to marry you?"

"You're right. That's on me. At that time, I was not in a good place, and I kept things from your mom. I slept with women in every town the Air Force sent me and I drank too much. I am not proud of that. She deserved a good guy, and back then, I was not." Danny paused. "If we had married back then, we would have divorced too. That was not something I wanted for you. I knew she had a son, and I know the pain of divorce," he said.

"Is that why you never had children with your wife, Lauren?" Freddy asked.

"No. When we got married, I stopped messing around. I was good with Lauren. She was one of the girls I was cheating on while dating your mom. Lauren could not have children. She had cancer when she was young and had surgery where she couldn't have kids. You see? It all worked out for the best. Your mom was right not to tell me about you. I don't blame her for that. She was right to find her husband, Freece. He sounds like a good man to raise you," Danny said.

"Well, I would like to meet you. If you are okay with that?" Freddy asked.

The two planned to meet and spend time together in Spring Mountain Valley. Freddy took pictures of the waterfalls they stood under and the mountainside they hiked. The two rode ATVs around Danny's property, and he helped his "Pop" with projects around the house. In the evenings, they sat under the night sky by a bonfire in the yard, while they continued their stories.

It was the night before Freddy would leave to come home that Danny asked, "What was your dad like?"

It had not gone without notice by Danny, that just a few months ago, Freddy had lost his father.

"My dad,? He was a good man. I didn't bring him up because I wasn't sure …"

"Oh no, you're fine. I don't want you to not talk about him around me. He was your dad. He raised you well, and I would like you to feel comfortable talking about him. Anytime you have a story, I'd like to hear it." Danny said.

Freddy gave a nod and a smile. It was still too soon for him to talk about Freece.

After a full three days, Danny stood outside on the front porch as Freddy drove down the long driveway. With a wave out the truck's window, he saw in the rearview mirror as his Pop gave a wave back.

That evening, once Freddy had arrived home, Elizabeth gave him the news. She was pregnant! That was the first year that Danny drove down for Christmas. At first, it was a little uncomfortable having him and Freddy in the same room with me. Watching Freddy laugh and joke with Danny warmed my heart. Freddy was fortunate to have both Freece and Danny in his life. Freece was there for the first 25 years, and now Danny could be there for the next.

The following February, they had a son, Joseph Freece Miles!

In the summer, Freddy, Elizabeth, and Joey went on their first family vacation to Spring Mountain Valley to be with Danny. They asked if I wanted to join them, but I explained, "My time with Danny is done. My heart will always be with Freece, and I never want to lose him inside of me. I am well and grateful for much. Watching the two of you raise your son gives me everything." I realized I had a love story that few could share. I had been given the opportunity to have loved twice! And now Freddy had that too!

I began spending more time with Freddy and Elizabeth. It gave me time to be with Joey. I finally understood what everyone was talking about in being a grandmother. It's truly a different type of love. Joey grew so fast in those first few months. I could see so much of Freddy in him.

The weekends were quiet once they had Joey.

On Sundays, we would gather at Freddy's house for dinner. Mama and Rico would come and, of course, she had a bag full of playing cards and her card shuffler.

"I just got off the phone with Pop," Freddy announced from the other room. "He's planning to come down again this year for Christmas."

"That'll be nice. And I have UNO," I shouted, laying down the DRAW FOUR card. "Sorry Elizabeth."

That was the Christmas when Danny came with an overload of Christmas gifts for everyone. And the day after, he dropped the bombshell about his cancer diagnosis. We had not realized that he had been dealing with the illness for a few years. He wasn't talking about it in detail, but he and Freddy went on with positive vibes of "we'll kick this." There had been so much loss in Freddy's life. I was worried for him.

When it was just the two of us alone, I shared with Freddy,
"Have you considered going to therapy or talking with a grief counselor?" After Freece passed away, my therapist referred me to a grief counselor who offered some great reading material.

"Being able to talk with her about Freece has really given healing to me. You may find that for yourself," I said, reminding me of when my mother said those words to me, years ago.

Danny stayed through the New Year as we all came together to bring in 2019!
Three weeks later, Freddy received a phone call …

Elizabeth

Freddy wanted to be there during Danny's last days. The sun was reaching out of the clouds that early, wintry morning. The TV played softly as the meteorologist announced, "No snow all winter, but it's making up for it today."

I snuggled up in my comfortable pants and oversized sweater, with a warm blanket over my legs, as I felt the cold from the window. The skies were gray with faint clouds to hide the sun, and I could see the flurries fall. Staring out this window, I had forgotten our reason for being here.

Freddy leaned in with a kiss to my forehead and glanced out the window.

"I see the snow is still falling. I only wish Dad could see it," he said.

"I know, babe. He has a pretty view."

Freddy sent a text to Danny's brother, Bentley. He asked him to notify other friends and family.

It had been two days since we'd arrived at the Hospice House, and it saddened me that today or tomorrow could be our last day with Danny. We took turns leaving the room for bathroom breaks or grabbing coffee. We didn't want to miss that he could open his eyes briefly or take his last breath.

Freddy received a text from Bentley.

"I'm stepping out to get Uncle Bentley. He's in the lobby."

I prepared myself for Uncle Bentley. With his reckless actions and crass words, he had always been a wild card.

Bentley entered the room with his voice raised.

"I tell you what, this Hospice House did a nice job on this place. The grounds and these rooms are comfortable for patients who are dying. We should ask if we can get a room with two beds, and I can stay. Have you tried this coffee? It's better than most."

Freddy told Bentley about the doctor's expectations for Danny. The nurses came in and explained that it was all right for us to stay as long as we wanted. They explained that based on his heart rate and response to the medication, "the time was getting close". Throughout the day, we constantly looked outside the window. If only he would open his eyes, he could take in this beautiful view. Through the curtain of snow falling, I saw a wooden gazebo in the distance, across the courtyard, its outline facing toward the lake. While Freddy and Bentley visited with Danny, I took some time to step away. I smelled the freshly brewed coffee as soon as I entered the hallway and made my way to the foyer, where donuts and a fresh pot were waiting. With no rush to go back and listen to Bentley, I saw a group of nurses standing at the front desk.

"How much snow do you think we'll get?" I asked.

"Well, if it doesn't stop, we may get snowed in," one nurse said.

I finished my donut, and that was my cue to walk away. "Have a nice day, ladies," I said as I raised my coffee.

I called Vivi to see how Joey was doing. We didn't know how long we would be there in Spring Mountain Valley. Leaving Joey with Vivi made the most sense. She could stay at the house to watch the dogs.

"How's Freddy doing?" Vivi asked.

"As expected. He has been holding it together, mostly. He mentioned last night how happy he was that they had this past year together."

"Yeah, these are the moments we realize how little time we all have together. Don't worry about us. Joey and I are doing great," Vivi said, offering comfort.

"Okay, I'll keep you updated if there are any changes." I hung up.

I couldn't help but think about how everyone spoke softly here as I walked down the hall. There was always a whisper. It truly gave that "peaceful feeling" and sense of calm in the air. I opened the door and walked inside to Bentley, discussing the stock market. He had changed the station to watch "his numbers" rise or fall.

"Elizabeth, what do you think of all this snow? You're a Florida girl, so you're not used to this weather," he said.

I looked at Freddy.

"How's he doing? I mean, how are you doing?" I asked.

Bentley changed the channel back to the local news and weather. The snow continued to fall, blanketing the grounds in a thick layer of white.

Being from Florida, I never got to see this type of beauty. On another day, I might have been tempted to go outside, lay in the snow, and let it fall on my face. I am still surprised to see the snowflakes on the window. They are such small pieces of art, each perfectly shaped. As I watched, each one fell and transformed into a tiny water drop.

"So, did your dad get to talk to you about his wishes for his house and property? Who is going to live in that big house now?" Bentley asked.

"Shh, lower your voice. He left all that information with his lawyer. I plan to take care of all that later," Freddy said.

Bentley could not help himself. "Well, take care of that sooner. You wouldn't want the family to come in and take what is not theirs."

I looked at Bentley and with my hand, gestured toward Danny. "Now is not the time."

"Well, if you need help, I live close by and can take care of that for you. I know you must travel from Florida each time," he said, still with his voice so loud.

"We don't mind the drive. It gives us a chance to get away. But thank you. I plan to follow whatever is written in his will," Freddy repeated.

That was when Bentley decided it was time for him to go. He approached Danny and leaned in.

"Alright, Danbo, I'm going to let you go now. I love you, brother. I'm going to miss you," he said, struggling to speak, his voice cracked.

He walked toward the door, and I followed him out.

"Bentley, come here."

And we hugged. He cried.

"Let me know when …" he trailed off, unable to say the words.

"I'll call you."

I stepped back inside Danny's room and saw Freddy was full of tears.

"Oh, babe. I am so sorry," I whispered as I held him.

"Why? Why did this have to happen to him? I finally found him, and now he's gone. We were just together three weeks ago. I want to talk to him. There's still so much to say," Freddy cried.

He was choking back more tears, and his words were drooling.

Daniel Robert Bullet, a United States Air Force military veteran, died on January 27, 2019.

He is preceded in death by his wife Lauren Johnson-Bullet.

He is survived by his son Frederick Miles, daughter-in-law, Elizabeth, and one grandson, Joseph Miles of Carroll Pines, Florida.

Lost Highway

Vivi

There were days when I needed to get out of the house and stretch my mind. I drove down Willowdale Road. It still gave me peace and comfort to drive down those streets. With the radio on high volume, *Lost Highway* by Bon Jovi seemed appropriate.

I remembered when Liv learned to drive on those streets, and she measured the distance from our mailbox to the bus stop intersection as 0.9 miles. I decided I'd have to let Freddy know that when I was a kid, "I walked a mile each way to and from the bus stop, rain, or shine."

I laughed at that.

As I drove, I realized the changes this street had taken. It had become a paved road, with matching concrete mailboxes lining both sides. The large pine trees still hovered over and allowed the Spanish moss to drip. I went down Half Moon Lake Road to the end, where Gator Lady lived, at the lake hole. Despite the overgrown bushes and grass, I could still see the pathway. Cliff Taylor's property was sold, and his house and trailers were gone. There stood a beautiful two-story home with white picket fencing surrounding the property.

Driving back to Willowdale Road, I saw they demolished Mr. Powell's house and sold the lot. Now, with no obstructions, I stopped there in front of our house and could see a clear view from where my bedroom window was directly across the street. I would have had a clear view of the lake.

Of course, there were no longer any hydrangeas or gardenias outside my bedroom window. They've since painted the house a dull tan color. I could still see the cinder blocks stacked the way Daddy placed them. The red bee tree in the front yard was gone.

Mr. Tim and Ms. Millie's trailer was no longer there, but a beautiful two-story home replaced it, with a circular driveway leading to the door. The garden was gone, but there was still a small shed in the distance. The tin roof showed rust and was smaller than I remember. I wondered if there was a bicycle to be made inside. Shannon's house was gone as well. The new owners had built on the backside of the property.

These memories were images in my mind as I remembered the people behind them.

As I drove by, I looked twice.

Mr. Cates was walking around the property alone. His house had stayed the same, but the bushes and trees were taller and fuller. I wouldn't stop—I should have—but I smiled instead. It was such a sweet feeling to see him still living there. Seeing the fence line still intact, where Baby would come to meet me each day.

I had my time here—this was my neighborhood. It was busy and active, with children riding bikes and climbing trees. Neighborhood boys played soccer in the field and rode minibikes through the orange groves.

Some houses were old, battered, or gone. They had built new homes, and young families had started a new story. The lake was still and quiet. It did not look like anyone swam or fished in this lake anymore. No boats or jet skis were causing ripples in the waters. I couldn't hear the kids' screams as they rode the waves and took their first stand on skis. While driving, I recognized the trees I used to climb as a kid. They were so much bigger now. I could feel them wave their long, sturdy branches at me as they bowed to greet me. Most people had passed on or moved away, but the trees still knew me, and I waved back.

I headed towards the circle where Carmen's house was. Later tonight, I would call her and let her know I'd passed by, and mention that the renters appeared to be neglecting the lawn. I was hoping she and Marc would move back.

I noticed that Mr. King's gates with the big K were gone, and the solid and sturdy bushes that created a wall of privacy had all but vanished. His house was now hidden by large, overgrown bougainvillea flowers and white birds of paradise palms covering its red brick face. The white fencing at the top of the house looked old and brittle. I could imagine him walking up there on his sundeck. The bold shutters that once secured the windows were damaged or disappeared.

I turned the corner, and it was as if a sign appeared up from the ground.

It read: FOR SALE.

My phone rang. *Freddy.*

I stopped alongside the road and glanced past the hammock on Mr. King's property; I stared out to that familiar view I had always dreamed of, there on Half Moon Lake.

"Hello, son. How are you?"

"Hey, Mom, what are you doing this weekend?"

And I told him everything.

"Well, I'm thinking of buying and renovating this property; I've had my eyes on it for a while now. You see, it has a sundeck …"

Acknowledgments

This book would never have been written without the residents of Willowdale Road. Your acts of kindness inspired this story.

To Mr. Tim, Ms. Mildred, the Bates, Mr. King, Mr. Powell, and even Gator Lady. **Thank you!**

To *Shannon, Rick, Wanda, and William,* you will forever be in my heart. **Thank you!**

To the team of editors and readers that kept my words in check. Your endless emails and motivation from the start were incredibly helpful. Ashleigh & Anna Lisa at Split Leaf Saturdays Editing, Dwain Cassady, Jane Ball, and Lisa Lee Editing.
Thank you!

To Kevin, Christian, Caleb, and Carmen, you are the ones who inspire me every single day. **Thank you!**
To my dog, Sofie, for sitting by my side during those tough chapters.

To Franc, thank you for being my biggest fan! Your continuous support and encouragement kept me going. x:

About the Author

Clara Bella Rose is from a small town near Tampa. Although she has lived in various states through the years, she always found her way back home to the Florida sunshine.

Traveling with her husband, riding fast roller coasters, and reaching her annual reading goal are among her favorite things.

Follow Clara at Instagram: @author.clarabellarose
Facebook: Clara Bella Rose
Email: Bell4roses@gmail.com

Willowdale Road is her debut novel.

HALF MOON LAKE is where Vivi returns to the neighborhood she knows best. She enjoys the view of the lake and takes pleasure in observing the neighbors—a habit that will bring her more than a thrill.
She never had a problem with keeping secrets until murder was involved.
Sometimes you do what you have to for the sake of the child.

There is more in the deep muck and mire of *Half Moon Lake* than what the ladies of Willowdale Road will tell.

Half Moon Lake - Coming soon, 2025!